My Friends

EMMANUEL BOVE

MY FRIENDS

translated from the French
by Janet Louth

CARCANET

First published in Great Britain 1986 by
Carcanet Press Ltd
208–212 Corn Exchange Buildings
Manchester M4 3BQ

Translation © 1986 Janet Louth
Mes Amis © Flammarion, 1977

British Library Cataloguing in Publication Data

Bove, Emmanuel
  My friends.
  I. Title   II. Mes amis. *English*
  843'.912[F]   PQ2603.087

  ISBN 0-85635-643-3

The publisher acknowledges the financial assistance
of the Arts Council of Great Britain

Typesetting by Paragon Photoset, Aylesbury
Printed in England by SRP Ltd, Exeter

CONTENTS

I

When I wake up, my mouth is open. My teeth are furry: it would be better to brush them in the evening, but I am never brave enough. Tears have dried at the corners of my eyes. My shoulders do not hurt any more. Some stiff hair covers my forehead. I spread my fingers and push it back. It is no good: like the pages of a new book it springs up and tumbles over my eyes again.

When I bow my head I can feel that my beard has grown: it pricks my neck.

I lie on my back, the back of my neck warm, my eyes open, the sheets up to my chin so that the bed will not get cold again.

The ceiling is stained with damp: it is very close to the roof. In places there are air-bubbles under the wallpaper. My furniture looks like the wares of a junk merchant out on the pavement. The pipe of my little stove is tied up with a rag, like a knee. At the top of the window a blind which no longer works hangs askew.

When I stretch out, I can feel the vertical bedrailings under the soles of my feet, a bit like a tightrope walker.

My clothes, resting heavily over my legs, are flat, warm on one side only. My shoe-laces no longer have any tags.

The room is cold as soon as it rains. You would not think anyone had slept there. Water, streaming down the window-panes, eats into the putty and forms a puddle on the ground.

When the sun blazes out, all alone in the sky, it throws its golden light into the middle of the room. The flies make a thousand straight lines on the floor.

Every morning, my neighbour sings wordlessly while she moves her furniture about. Her voice is deadened by the wall. I feel as if I am behind a gramophone.

I often meet her on the stairs. She works in a dairy. At nine o'clock she comes to do her housework. Her felt slippers are stained with drops of milk.

I like women in slippers: their legs seem more accessible.

In summer her breasts and the shoulder-straps of her camisole show through her blouse.

I have told her that I love her. She laughed, no doubt because I am not good-looking and am poor. She prefers men in uniform. She has been seen with her hand under the white belt of a *garde républicain*.

Another room is occupied by an old man. He is seriously ill: he has a cough. There is a lump of rubber at the end of his walking-stick. His shoulder-blades make two projections on his back. A prominent vein runs across his temple, between skin and bone. His jacket does not touch his hips any more: it swings out as if the pockets were empty. The poor man climbs the stairs one by one, holding on to the hand-rail. As soon as I see him I breathe in as deeply as possible so that I can pass him without taking another breath.

On Sundays his daughter visits him. She is very smart. Her coat lining looks like the feathers of a parrot. It is so splendid that I wonder if the coat is inside out. As for her hat, it must have cost a lot, because to protect it, she takes a taxi when it is raining. This lady smells of scent, real scent, not one of the cheap varieties.

The tenants of my house cannot bear her. They say

that instead of leading a life of luxury she would do better to relieve her father's poverty.

The Lecoin family also lives on my landing.

At dawn their alarm-clock rings.

The husband does not like me. I am polite to him all the same. He holds it against me that I get up late.

He comes home at about seven o'clock every evening, with his working clothes rolled up under his arm and smoking an English cigarette — which makes people say that labourers are doing very nicely.

He is tall and brawny. It is possible to make use of his strength, if one pays him compliments. Last year he carried a trunk down for a woman on the third floor, with some difficulty, it is true, because the lid would not close.

When people speak to him, he stares at them, because he thinks they are making fun of him. At the hint of a smile he says: 'You see . . . four years of war . . . The Germans didn't get me . . . You won't get me today . . .'

One day as he passed me he muttered: 'Lazy bugger!' I went pale and did not know what to reply. I could not sleep for a week because I was afraid I had an enemy. I imagined that he was looking for an opportunity to get at me and was deadly jealous of me.

All the same, if Monsieur Lecoin only knew how I like people who work, how sorry I feel for their way of life! If he knew what I have to go without to maintain my little independence!

He has two daughters and he beats them — just with his hand — for their own good. They have sinews at the back of their knees. Their hats are held on by elastic.

I like children, so I greet these two girls when I meet them. Then they turn round and suddenly, without replying, they run away.

Every Tuesday Madame Lecoin does her washing

on the landing. The tap runs all day. As the big jugs fill up, the sound changes. Mme Lecoin's skirt is old-fashioned. Her bun is so scanty you can see all the hair-pins.

She often stares at me, but I do not trust her, for it seems very likely she is setting a trap for me. Anyway, she has no breasts.

I get out of the sheets and sit on the edge of the bed. My legs hang down from the knees. The pores of my thighs are black. My toenails are long and sharp: a stranger would find them ugly.

I stand up. My head spins, but the giddiness rapidly disappears. When it is sunny, a cloud of dust from the bed sparkles for a minute in the rays, like rain.

First I put on my socks; if I did not, matches would stick to the soles of my feet. I put on my trousers holding on to a chair.

Before I put on my shoes, I examine the soles to see how long they are likely to last.

Then I put my wash-basin, which is ringed by the previous day's dirty water, on top of the slop bucket. I am in the habit of washing in a stooping position, with legs apart, my braces attached only by the back buttons. When I was in the army I used to wash like that in the narrow mess-tin. My basin is so small that the water over-flows it if I put both hands in at once. My soap does not lather any more: it is so thin.

I use the same towel for my face and for my hands. It would be just the same if I were rich.

I feel better once I have washed. I breathe through my nose. My teeth are clean. My hands will stay clean until midday.

I put on my hat. The brim has been put out of shape by the rain. The ribbon is fashionably knotted at the back.

I hang up my looking-glass on the window. I like looking at myself in full light. I look better. My cheeks, nose and chin are lit up. The rest is in shadow. It is as if I were having my photograph taken in the sun.

I have to take care not to get too far away from the mirror, because its quality is poor. At a distance it distorts my reflection.

I examine my nostrils carefully, and the corners of my eyes, and my back teeth. They are decayed. They are not falling out: they are crumbling. With the help of another mirror I catch sight of my profile. Then it feels as if there were two of me. Film actors must be familiar with this pleasure.

Then I open my window. The door shakes. A First World War print rattles against the wall. I can hear people shaking carpets. I see blue zinc roofs, chimney-stacks, a mist which shivers when a sunbeam pierces it.

Before going out, I cast an eye over my room. My bed is already cold. There are some feathers sticking out of the eiderdown. The legs of my chair have holes where the stretchers should be. The two leaves of a round table hang down.

This furniture belongs to me. A friend made me a present of it before he died. I disinfected it myself with sulphur, because I am afraid of contagious illnesses. I was frightened for a long time in spite of this precaution. I want to stay alive.

I put on my overcoat with some difficulty, because the lining of the sleeves is coming unstitched.

I put my military pass-book, my key and my dirty handkerchief which crackles when I unfold it into my left pocket. I have one shoulder higher than the other: the weight of these objects helps to bring it lower.

The door does not open properly. In order to get out I do up my coat and go through sideways.

The tiled floor of the landing is broken. A strip of

metal, with three holes, hangs from the window-frame. The hand-rail ends in the wall, without a knob.

I go down the stairs, hugging the wall where the steps are wider. I do not hold the rail in order not to get my hands dirty. Bunches of keys swing from the key-holes.

I am light-hearted as if I were going out without my overcoat for the first time. My eyelashes and the inside of my ears are still damp with washing-water. I am sorry for people who are still asleep.

I always see the concierge. She has put the doormats over the banister while she sweeps a landing, or else she brushes a corridor with a yellow broom. I say 'Good morning'. She scarcely replies and gazes at my shoes.

She would like to be alone in the house after eight o'clock.

II

I live in Montrouge.

The new blocks of flats in my street still smell of cut stone.

My own house is not new. The plaster on the front is falling off in bits. There is a rail across the windows. The top floor has no ceiling, just the roof. The shutters are hooked back against the wall when it is not windy. The architect did not carve his name above the number.

In the morning the street is quiet.

A concierge is sweeping, but only in front of her own door.

When I pass her, I breathe through my nose because of the dust.

Through the open windows, I can see some potted plants which have just been watered, the copper fittings and the narrow, polished strips of parquet flooring, forming zigzags.

I am embarrassed when my eyes meet those of a tenant.

Sometimes there is a white cloth moving behind a curtain, at a man's height: somebody is having a wash.

I have my coffee near where I live, in a small café. The zinc counter is wavy at the edge. The wooden floor, which is washed without soap, seems very old. A gramophone, which used to work before the war, is turned to the wall. People wonder what it is doing there, as it does not work.

The proprietor is pleasant. He is small like a soldier at the tail-end of a platoon. He has a glass eye which is so like the real one, that I never know which is which — and this bothers me. It seems to me that he is annoyed when I look at his artificial eye.

He told me that he had been wounded in the war: but people say he was already blind in one eye in 1914.

The worthy man is always complaining. Trade is falling off. It is no good for him to polish the glasses in front of customers; it is no good for him to say: 'Thank you, sir; goodbye, sir; never mind the door', nobody comes.

He would like the war to be forgotten. He is sorry it is no longer 1910.

At that time, according to him, people were decent and friendly. The army looked like the army. It was possible to give credit. People were interested in social problems.

When he speaks of all this, both his eyes — the real and the artificial — become moist and his eyelashes stick together.

The time before the war vanished so quickly that he cannot believe it is nothing but a memory.

We too tackle social problems. He attaches great importance to doing that. It proves to his own satisfaction that the war has not changed him.

Every day he assures me that in Germany, a better organized country than ours, there are no beggars. The French authorities ought to prohibit begging.

'But it is prohibited!'

'Oh, come on! Look at all those tramps selling bootlaces! They are richer than you and me.'

As I do not like arguments, I take care not to reply. I swallow my coffee, made brown by a drop of milk, pay and go out.

'See you tomorrow!' he calls, as he puts my still warm cup under a trickle of water that can only be turned off from the cellar.

Farther on there is a grocer's shop.

The owner knows me. He is so fat that his apron is shorter in front than behind. His skin can be seen under his crew-cut. His American-style moustache blocks his nostrils and must stop him breathing through his nose.

In front of his shop there is a display — a small one, which is sensible — of sacks of lentils, prunes and jars of sweets. He comes out to serve, but does the weighing inside.

Formerly he used to chat to me when he stood on his door-step. He used to ask me if I would like anything, or else tell me that I looked in excellent health. He would go back into the shop with a gesture of his hand which meant: 'Until next time'.

One day he asked me to help him carry a box. I should have been glad to do so, but I have always been afraid of ruptures.

I refused, mumbling:

'I am not very strong, I was badly wounded.'

He has never spoken a word to me since.

There is also a butcher's shop in my street.

Quarters of meat hang by a tendon from silver hooks. The butcher's block is worn down in the middle like a step. Fillets of beef tied up with string bleed on to yellow paper. Sawdust sticks to the customers' feet. The polished weights are arranged in order of size. There are bars at the windows, as if someone feared that the meat might escape.

In the evening I see through these bars, which are painted red, some potted plants on the empty marble of the shop-window.

The proprietor of this butcher's does not remember me: I have only ever bought four sous' worth of scraps for a flea-ridden cat and that was last year.

The baker's is very well looked after. A girl washes the shop front every morning. Water trickles down the sloping pavement.

Through the window the whole shop can be seen, with its mirrors, its Louis XV woodwork and its cakes on wire trays.

Although only people who are well-off frequent this baker's, I am one of its customers too — bread costing the same price everywhere.

I often stop in front of a shop where the boys of the neighbourhood buy caps.

Outside on a table there are some newspapers folded so that only half of their titles can be read.

The *Excelsior* alone is hanging up like a table-cloth.

I look at the pictures. The over-sized photographs always show the same thing: a boxing-ring or a re-volver with its cartridge-cases.

As soon as the shop-keeper sees me coming, she comes out of her shop. A smell of painted toys and new cotton comes with her.

She is old and thin. The lenses of her spectacles look like magnifying-glasses. Her meagre bun is imprisoned in a hair-net. Her lips have retreated permanently into her mouth. Her black apron fits tightly over a stomach which seems to be in the wrong place. She disappears into the back room to change five francs.

I ask her how she is.

It would be extremely rude not to reply; so she shakes her head. She has left the door open, so I can see she is waiting for me to go.

One day I picked up a paper to read the small type.

She said in an ill-natured voice:

'That's three sous.'

I wanted to tell her that I had been in the war, that I had been badly wounded, that I had won a service medal, that I was receiving a pension, but I immediately saw that it would be no good.

As I left, I heard the door closing with the noise of a scraping mudguard.

I have to go past the dairy where my neighbour works. This embarrasses me, because I am sure she has not kept my declaration of love to herself. People must be laughing at me.

So I walk quickly, picking out in a rapid glance pats of butter scored with wire, pictures of the countryside on the lids of the Camembert and a net put over the eggs, because of thieves.

III

When a longing for luxury comes over me I go and walk around near the Madeleine. It is a wealthy district. The streets smell of wood-block paving and exhaust-fumes. The swirling air behind the buses and taxis buffets my face and hands. In front of the cafés the rapid rise and fall of voices seem to come from a revolving megaphone. I look at the parked cars. The women leave a trail of scent behind them in the air. I only cross the road when a policeman is holding up the traffic.

It seems to me that the people sitting at tables on the terraces notice me in spite of my shabby clothes.

Once a woman sitting behind a tiny tea-pot eyed me from head to foot.

Happy and full of hope, I retraced my steps. But the customers smiled and the waiter looked at me hard.

For a long time I remembered that unknown woman, her throat and her breasts. I undoubtedly pleased her.

When I was in bed and heard midnight striking, I was sure she was thinking about me.

Oh, how I should love to be rich!

Everyone would admire the fur collar of my over-coat, especially in the suburbs. My jacket would be open. A gold chain would hang across my waistcoat; my purse would be attached to my braces by a silver chain. I should carry my wallet in my revolver pocket,

as Americans do. I should have to make an elegant
gesture in order to look at the time on my wrist-watch.
I should put my hands in my jacket pockets, with the
thumbs outside, and not, like the *nouveaux riches*, in the
arm-holes of my waistcoat.

I should have a mistress, an actress.

We should go, she and I, to have an apéritif on the
terrace of the largest café in Paris. The waiter would
roll away the pedestal tables like barrels to make way
for us. Ice-cubes would float in our glasses. The cane of
the chairs would not be coming to bits.

We should have dinner in a restaurant where there
were table-cloths and flowers elegantly arranged.

She would go in first. Polished mirrors would reflect
my form a hundred times, like a row of lamp-posts.
When the manager bowed his greeting to us, his
starched shirt-front would bulge from the waist to the
collar. The solo violinist would sway backwards and
forwards as if on a spring-board, balancing his body.
Locks of hair would flop over his eyes, as if he had just
come out of a bath.

At the theatre we should have a box. I should be able to
touch the curtain if I leaned forward. All round the
auditorium people would look at us through opera
glasses.

All of a sudden the footlights behind their zinc
screen would light up the stage.

We should have a sideways view of the stage-set
and, in the wings, actors not moving a muscle.

A fashionable singer, with jet buttons, would throw
us a glance after each couplet.

Then a dancer would spin round on her pointes. The
yellow, red and green spotlights which followed her

would fall unevenly like the colouring of a picture by Épinal.

In the morning we should go by taxi to the Bois de Boulogne.

The driver's elbows would move.

Through the shuddering glass of the windows we should see people standing still and others who seemed to be walking slowly.

Skidding round a bend, the taxi would throw us from our places and then we should kiss.

When we arrived, I should get out first, lowering my head, then I should give my companion my hand.

I should pay without looking at the meter. I should leave the door open.

Passers-by would watch us. I should pretend not to see them.

I should receive my mistress in my bachelor's flat on the ground floor of a new house. The building's plate-glass door would be protected by flat, wrought-iron palm-branches. The bell-push would glitter in the middle of its bronze surround. The mahogany of a lift at the end of the corridor would be visible from the doorway.

I should have had a shower in the morning. My linen would smell freshly ironed. Two of my waistcoat buttons would be undone, making me look relaxed.

My mistress would arrive at three o'clock.

I should take off her hat. We should sit on a sofa. I should kiss her hands, her elbows and her shoulders.

Then we should make love.

My mistress would throw herself back, drunk with passion. Her eyes would become glazed. I should unfasten her dress. To please me, she would be wearing a chemise with lace on it.

Then, murmuring endearments, she would give herself up to me, moistening my chin with her kisses.

Lucie Dunois

Sometimes I eat at the soup-kitchen in the fifth arrondissement. Unfortunately it does not suit me because there are too many of us. We have to arrive in good time. Then we queue up for I don't know how long, beside a wall, on the pavement. The passers-by stare at us. It is very disagreeable.

I prefer the little wine-shop in the rue de la Seine, where I am known. The owner is called Lucie Dunois. Her name, in enamelled capital letters, is stuck on to the glass of the shop-window. Three letters are missing.

Lucie has a beer-drinker's figure. An aluminium ring — a souvenir of her husband who died at the front — decorates the index finger of her right hand. Her ears are flabby. Her shoes have no heels. She keeps blowing at the wisps of hair which have escaped from her bun. When she bends over, her skirt splits open at the back like a chestnut. Her pupils are not in the middle of her eyes; they are too high up, like those of alcoholics.

The room smells of empty barrels, rats and slops. Above the gas-mantle there is an asbestos fan which does not turn. In the evening the gas-lamp throws its light right under the tables. A notice — Regulations on the Control of Drunkenness — is nailed to the wall, where it can be seen clearly. A few pages are sticking out of the printed slab of a street-directory. A stained mirror, scratched on the back, decorates the partition wall.

I eat at one o'clock, to make the afternoon seem shorter.

Two masons in white smocks, their cheeks smudged with plaster, are drinking coffee, which, by contrast, seems absolutely black.

I settle myself in a corner, as far as possible from the entrance: I hate sitting near a door. Some workmen have been eating at my place. The table is littered with the wrapper of a *petit suisse* and some egg-shells.

Lucie is nice to me. She serves me with a steaming bowl of soup, some fresh crumbly bread, a plate of vegetables and sometimes a bit of meat.

When I have finished my meal, grease congeals on my lips.

Every three months, when I receive my pension, I give Lucie a hundred francs. She cannot make much out of me.

In the evening I wait until all the customers have gone, because I am the one who shuts up the eating-house. I always hope Lucie will keep me.

Once she did tell me to stay.

When I had lowered the metal shutter with a pole, I crawled back into the café on all fours. Finding myself in a shop which was closed to the public felt very strange. I did not feel at home.

My excitement soon got rid of these feelings.

Now I gazed more indulgently at the woman who would certainly become my mistress. She would not please most men, but all the same she was a woman, with big breasts and hips wider than mine. And she must like me, because she had asked me to stay.

Lucie uncorked a dusty bottle, washed her hands

with household soap and came and sat down opposite me.

Grease was still shining on her ring and round her nails.

In spite of myself, I was listening to the noises in the street.

We were embarrassed because we were not as well acquainted as the all too obvious object of my presence there suggested.

'Let's have a drink,' she said, wiping the neck of the bottle with her apron.

We chatted for an hour.

I should have liked to kiss her, if I had not had to go round the table to do it. It would be better to wait for a more favourable opportunity, especially for the first time.

Suddenly she asked me if I had ever seen her room.

Of course I replied:

'No.'

We stood up. A shiver made me hug myself. She lit a candle before she put out the gas. The drops of wax which fell on her fingers hardened at once. She flicked them off with a nail, without breaking them.

The candle-flame wavered in the kitchen, and then flattened as we climbed the stairs, as steep as a ladder, which led to her bedroom.

With nothing in my mind I followed her, instinctively walking on my toes.

She lowered the candle to light up the key-hole, then she opened the door.

The shutters of her room were closed, as they had been all day no doubt. The bed-clothes were hanging on the back of a chair. I could see the red-striped mattress. The wardrobe was half open. I thought Lucie's savings must be there, under a pile of under-clothes. I looked tactfully in another direction.

She showed me the enlargements of photographs decorating the walls and then she sat down on the bed. I joined her.

'How do you like my room?'

'Very much.'

Suddenly, as if to prevent her falling, I clasped her to me. She did not defend herself. Encouraged by this I kissed her a thousand times, while I undressed her with one hand. I wanted to rip her button-holes and tear her clothing, as great lovers do, but I was afraid she would have something to say about it if I did.

Soon she was in her corset. The whalebones were twisted. It was laced up at the back. Her breasts were touching.

I trembled as I unfastened her corset. Her chemise stuck to her body for a moment and then dropped.

I had difficulty in taking it off, because the narrow neck would not go over her shoulders. I left her with only her stockings on, because I think that looks more attractive. Besides, in the papers, the nudes always wear stockings.

At last she was naked. Her thighs bulged out over her garters. Her spine dented her skin in the small of her back. She had been vaccinated on the arms.

I lost my head. Shivers like those which make horses' legs tremble ran up and down my body.

The next morning, at about five o'clock, Lucie woke me. She was already dressed. I did not dare meet her eye because I do not look my best early in the morning.

'Hurry up, Victor, I must go down.'

Although I was half asleep, I understood at once that she did not want to leave me alone in her room: she did not trust me.

I dressed quickly and, without washing, followed her on to the stairs.

She locked her door.

'Go and raise the metal shutter.'

I did as she said then I sat down, hoping she would offer me a cup of coffee.

'You had better go, the customers will be arriving.'

Although she was now my mistress, I went away without asking for anything.

Since then, whenever I go there to eat, she serves me just as she always has done, no better and no worse.

Henri Billard

I

Being alone is hard to bear. I should like to have a friend, a real friend, or else a mistress to whom I could tell all my troubles.

When you wander about all day without speaking to anyone, you feel so tired in your room in the evening.

For a little affection, I should share everything I possess: my pension money, my bed. I should be so considerate of anyone who showed me any friendship. I should never contradict them. All their wishes would be mine. I should follow them everywhere, like a dog. I should laugh at all their jokes; if anyone grieved them, I should cry.

I am endlessly kind. But the people I have known have never appreciated this fact.

Billard no more than the rest.

I got to know Henri Billard in a crowd in front of a pharmacy.

Crowds in the street always make me nervous. This is because I am afraid of finding myself in the presence of a corpse. Nevertheless, a necessity which does not come from curiosity drives me forward. Even though I am afraid of what I may see, I force my way through, in spite of myself. Not a word those onlookers say escapes me: I try to find out what is happening before I look.

One evening, at about six o'clock, I found myself in a throng of people, so close to the policeman who was holding them back that I could make out the ship of the city of Paris on his silver-gilt buttons. The people behind me were pushing, as always happens when a crowd is gathering.

Inside the shop, next to the scales, a man was sitting, unconscious, but with his eyes open. He was so small that the nape of his neck rested on the back of the chair and his legs hung down like a pair of stockings drying toes down. From time to time his eyes swivelled in their sockets. The front of his trousers was covered with a great number of shiny stains. His jacket was fastened with a pin.

The chemist's air of concern, the low opinion the onlookers had of the poor man's clothes and the interest which he was arousing struck me as unusual.

A woman wrapped in a thick shawl looked about her and murmured:

'It's a fainting fit.'

'Don't push . . . don't push,' advised an elderly man.

A shop-keeper who was keeping an eye on the open door of her establishment said for the information of all and sundry:

'Everybody knows him in this district. He's a dwarf. Really poor people are proud; they don't draw attention to themselves. There's nothing remarkable about that man: he drinks.'

It was then that my neighbour, to whom I had paid no attention before, remarked:

'If he drinks, he's right.'

This opinion pleased me, but if I agreed it was barely enough for this unknown to notice it.

'That's what comes of over-indulgence,' said a gentleman holding a pair of gloves with beautifully smoothed-out fingers.

'Until the revolution cleans up modern society there are bound to be unhappy wretches about,' declared an old man quietly, the one who had just been advising people not to push.

The policeman, whose cape made him look rather odd because it hid his arms, turned round, and the onlookers exchanged glances which showed that they did not share the opinions of this Utopian.

'They all end up like this,' mumbled a housewife whose false teeth had momentarily come out of place.

A man who, without knowing it, was imitating the grimaces of the dwarf, nodded approvingly.

'Why don't you send him to hospital?' I asked the policeman.

I could have obtained the information from one of my neighbours; but no, I preferred to question the officer. It seemed to me that, in this way, the rigour of the law was relaxed for me alone.

The dwarf had closed his eyes. His stomach heaved with his breathing. His sleeves and shoe-laces were agitated by regular shudders. A trickle of saliva ran down his chin. Beneath his half-open shirt a small, pointed nipple could be seen, looking as if it were wet.

The poor man was certainly going to die.

I cast a sidelong glance at my neighbour. His moustache was curled. His shirt collar was fastened with a gilt stud. Thin, small and energetic, he very much appealed to me, because I am tall, lazy and emotional.

Night was falling. The gas-lamps were already lit, but not yet giving any light. The sky was a cold blue. The map-like markings of the moon stood out clearly. My neighbour went off without saying good-bye. His hesitant manner seemed to give an indication that he wanted me to join him.

I held back for a second, as anyone in my position would have done, for, after all, I did not know him; the police could easily be looking for him.

Then, without thinking, I caught him up.

The distance had been so short that I did not have time to prepare what I was going to say. Not a word came from my mouth. As for the stranger, he was not bothering about me.

He walked in a curious way, putting his heel down before his sole like a black man. There was a cigarette behind his ear.

I was vexed with myself for having followed him; but I live alone, I do not know anyone. Friendship would be such a great comfort to me.

Now it was impossible for me to leave him, because we were walking along next to each other in the same direction.

All the same, at a street corner I wanted to run away. As soon as I was gone, he could have thought what he liked of me. But I did not do anything.

'Have you got a cigarette?' he asked suddenly.

I glanced instinctively at his ear but quickly lowered my eyes in order not to offend him.

In my opinion he should have smoked his own cigarette first. Of course he could have forgotten about it.

I gave him a cigarette.

He lit it without enquiring if I had any left and went on walking. I still followed him, his lack of attention making me embarrassed in front of the passers-by. I wished he would turn towards me or ask me a question, which would have enabled me to know how to take him.

The cigarette I had given him had established a relationship between us. I could no longer go away; besides I prefer to put up with embarrassment rather than be rude.

'Come and have a drink,' he said, stopping in front of a bar.

I refused, not out of politeness, but because I was afraid he would not pay. This trick had been played on me before. It is important to be careful, especially with strangers.

He insisted.

I had a little money with me, should he slip away; so I went in.

The proprietor, who was sitting down like a customer, quickly went back behind the counter.

'Good evening, gentlemen.'

'Good evening, Jacob.'

The ceiling of the room was low, like that of a railway carriage. There were some cheap cinema tickets on the till.

My companion ordered a beer.

'What do you want?'

'The same as you.'

I wanted to ask for a liqueur, but my idiotic shyness prevented me.

My neighbour swallowed a mouthful of beer, then, wiping the froth from his moustache, he asked:

'What's your name?'

'Bâton, Victor,' I replied, as I used to do in the army.

'Bâton?'

'Yes.'

'What a name!' he said, imitating the action of somebody whipping up a horse.

I was no stranger to this little joke, but I was very surprised to come across it in a man who seemed so reserved.

'And you, what is your name?'

'Henri Billard.'

If I had not been afraid of offending him, I should have made a joke of his name too, by pretending to play billiards.

My companion opened his purse and paid.

I was not thirsty, so I found it difficult to finish my beer.

Suddenly the idea of offering him a drink came to me. I struggled against it. After all, I did not know Billard. But at the thought of finding myself alone in the street I weakened.

I emptied my head of every thought so that nothing could hold me back, and said in a voice which sounded to me as if I was talking to myself:

'Please . . . do let me get you a drink.'

There was a silence. I waited nervously for him to reply, fearful of either yes or no.

At last he answered:

'Why should you spend your money on me? You are poor, aren't you?'

I stammered out a repetition of my offer: it was no good.

Billard went out slowly, swinging his arms and limping slightly, no doubt because he had been standing still for so long. I copied him, limping for no reason.

'Good-bye, Bâton.'

I do not like leaving somebody with whom I have been getting on well without finding out his address or when I shall see him again. When this does happen, in spite of all my efforts, I feel uneasy for several hours. I am haunted by thoughts of death, which I usually chase away as quickly as possible. This person, going away for ever, reminded me, I do not know why, that I should die alone.

I looked sadly at Billard.

'Well, good-bye, Bâton.'

'You're going?'

'Yes.'

'Perhaps I shall see you round here again.'

'Oh, yes.'

I went home thoughtfully. Billard must indeed be a kind man to have refused my offer. He must certainly like and understand me.

People who like me a little and understand me are so hard to find.

II

The next day, when I woke up, I thought of him at once. As I lay in bed, I went over the details of our meeting. I could not remember Billard's face properly. It was in vain that I called to mind his moustache, hair and nose; his expression was always missing.

How happy I should be if he were my friend! We should go out in the evening. We should eat together. If I were short of money, he would lend me some and the other way round, too, of course. I should introduce him to Lucie. Life is so miserable for someone who is alone and speaks only to people who take no interest in him.

The day passed slowly. In spite of all the noises in the city, I heard every hour strike, as one does during a sleepless night. I could only wait. Frequent cold sweats made me feel there must be a draught between my shirt and my body.

In the afternoon I went for a walk in a park.

As I can read Roman numbers, I entertained myself by working out the age of the statues. Each time I was disappointed: they were never more than a hundred years old. It was not long before my polished shoes were covered with dust. Children's hoops spun round on the spot before tumbling down. People were sitting back to back on the benches.

Everything I saw provided distraction only for my eyes. Inside my head there was always Billard.

At last the evening came. I went along the streets where Billard and I had walked. The pharmacy was deserted. This seemed very strange to me because in my mind it was associated with a crowd of people.

Nothing prevented me from hanging about in the neighbourhood of the Café Jacob earlier on, but I knew that if I were to meet Billard at the same time as on the previous day, it would be less obvious that I had been looking for him. He would think I passed that way about six o'clock every day.

The café was not far away. My pounding heart made me aware of the shape of the left side of my chest. I kept wiping my damp hands on my sleeves. A smell of sweat escaped through my open jacket.

I imagined that the proprietor would be behind his counter and Billard drinking his beer, as they had been yesterday.

I stood on my toes, my hand against the window to steady myself, and looked over a red curtain into the Café Jacob.

Billard was not there.

I felt a surge of resentment. I had supposed that, as he liked me, he would have come back in the hope of speaking to me.

I looked at the clock on a baker's shop. It stood at six o'clock. All was not lost: Billard could be at work.

I went away, deciding to come back twenty minutes later. He would certainly be there then. We should talk; I had so many things to tell him.

To kill time, I wandered along a nearby street. The trees, with iron railings round the trunk, seemed to be standing upright like lead soldiers. I could see the passengers in the lighted trams. Taxis, dark and stubby, jolted over the paving-stones. Two flashing signs no longer attracted attention because they went on and off so regularly.

For half an hour I looked at the prices of shoes, ties and hats. I stopped in front of jewellers' shops too. The tiny price-tags were upside-down. It is impossible to find out the price of watches and rings without going into the shops.

By now Billard must be waiting for me, because he did really care about me, for if he did not he would not have offered me a beer.

I was suddenly afraid he might have come and gone again, so I went quickly back to the Café Jacob.

I was glad night had fallen. The proprietor and customers would not see me in the dark. I should study them from the street, and if Billard was not there, they would not be able to see the disappointment on my face.

The hundred metres which I still had to cover seemed endless. I wanted to break into a run, but was afraid of making myself look ridiculous: I have never run in the street. Besides, I run as badly as a woman.

At last I arrived in front of the bar. I lit a cigarette and then peered inside.

Billard was not there.

I was seized with a fit of dizziness which made me see three of everything, each passer-by and house and vehicle.

I realize that some people might well have laughed at my emotion. Nothing of what had happened would have made such an impression on anyone but me. I am too sensitive and that is all there is to it.

A minute later I went away completely downcast. Instead of pulling myself together, I tried to prolong my misery. I withdrew into myself, making myself more insignificant and wretched than I really am. In that way I found some comfort in my sorrows.

Billard had not come.

There have always been people like that in my life. Nobody has ever responded to my love. All I ask is to be allowed to love, to have some friends — and I always live alone. People do me some kindness, then they run away. I have never had any real luck.

I gulped down my saliva to stop myself crying.

I was walking straight ahead, a fresh cigarette between my lips, when I saw a man standing by a lamp-post. I thought at first it was a beggar, because they often stand about.

Suddenly a cry broke from me, as involuntarily as a hiccup.

The man was Billard. He had on a shabby overcoat such as down-and-outs wear. Near the street-lamp, in the dim light it provided, he was rolling a cigarette.

'Hallo, Monsieur Billard.'

He turned, looked at me and did not recognize me, which put me out. However, I immediately forgave his failing to remember me. It was a murky night. His eyes were dazzled by the light of the gas-lamp and he could not see me properly.

'It's me, Bâton.'

He licked his cigarette paper carefully.

I waited and, so that he should not see that I was smoking a ready-made cigarette, I stubbed it out on the wall and put it in my pocket.

'Where are you eating?' he asked.

'Where am I eating?'

'Yes.'

'Oh, anywhere.'

'Come with me; I know a cheap restaurant.'

I followed him. When I walk next to anyone, without meaning to, I push him towards the wall: so I watched myself carefully. As soon as the pavement grew narrow, I stepped down on to the road. As he was muttering I kept turning towards him, because I thought he was speaking to me: I did not want him to feel that I did not care about him.

The pleasure of having found Billard again took away my appetite. Although I was tormented by the desire to speak about myself, my neighbours, my life, I could not get a word out. I was completely paralysed with shyness, apart from my eyes. It is true that I did not know my companion very well.

No doubt he had hundreds of things he wanted to tell me about too, but, like me, he did not dare. Under his rough exterior he was a sensitive man.

'I have bought a Camembert. We'll share it. I usually have dinner with my wife. She's away today.'

'So, you're married?'

'No, we just live together.'

My good humour vanished immediately. A dozen thoughts at a time chased through my brain.

I remembered my room, Lucie, my street. The future appeared as a procession of days all the same. Yes, I held it against Billard that he had a woman. We could no longer be united in real friendship because a third person would be in the way. I was jealous. So, why had I followed this stranger? He had disconcerted me. Loneliness would weigh on me more heavily because of him.

All these thoughts did not stop me from hanging on to a last hope. Perhaps his mistress was not beautiful! She had only to be ugly for me to be able to pull myself together.

'Is she pretty?' I asked, trying hard to make myself sound casual.

With all the confidence of a coarse-natured person he replied that she was magnificent and had well-developed breasts, even though she was only eighteen. He even rounded his hands and showed me what they were like.

This time, I had only one idea: to go away. The injustice of fate was indeed too great. Billard had a wart and flat feet and yet someone loved him, while I lived alone, even though I was younger and better-looking.

We should never be able to understand each other. He was happy. As a result, I was of no interest to him. It would be better for me to go away.

We were still walking. I was looking for an excuse to get myself away. How I should have liked to be sitting, humble, alone and sad, in a corner of the restaurant in the rue de la Seine! There, at least, nobody would be bothering about me.

Indeed, Billard had no tact. If I had been married, I should not have said that. He ought to have known that people do not boast of their happiness to somebody who is miserable.

Nevertheless, I could not make up my mind to leave my companion. An encouraging thought was growing up in the depths of my mind. It could be that this woman did not love Billard. Perhaps he was unhappy! How deeply I should feel for him then! I should comfort him. Friendship would make our sufferings less harsh.

But, as I was afraid he would tell me she did, I took good care not to ask him if his mistress loved him.

'What's the matter? Are you unhappy?' he asked.

My misery, which had gone on increasing until that moment, vanished. The interest which Billard took in me was real, whereas my thoughts were nothing but the wanderings of a wretchedly dejected man.

I looked at him gratefully.

'Yes, I'm unhappy.'

I expected him to confide his troubles to me. I was disappointed: he advised me to pull myself together.

We stopped before a restaurant. The paint was

peeling off the front. On one of the windows the passers-by could read: 'Customers may bring their own food.'

'Go in,' said Billard.

I pushed down the door-handle and the chain rattled. Several people turned round.

I stopped on the threshold.

'Go in, then!'

'No, you go first.'

He went in in front of me. At that moment it occurred to me that I was the one who had opened and closed the door.

The room was furnished with long tables and some of those refectory benches which go up at one end when one sits down. Tobacco-smoke spiralled upwards, like syrup in a glass of water. The trap-door to the cellar trembled under our feet. Before each customer stood a bottle and glass. It would have been possible to play tunes on them with a knife.

We settled ourselves facing each other.

Billard tried to get the Camembert out of his pocket which was narrow. He had to use both hands.

Then, as a regular customer, he summoned the proprietress by her Christian name:

'Maria.'

She was a handsome countrywoman who kept on wiping her fore-arms with a cloth. Her breasts shook when she walked and the small change jingled in her apron pocket.

'Two half-litres and some bread.'

'Half a litre is too much for me,' I said, rather late.

'It's all right . . . I'm paying.'

'But you are not well off.'

'Just this once. It doesn't mean I'll always do it.'

I had no wish to take advantage of my neighbour's kindness. That is why what he said shook me so profoundly. I shall never find such a good and generous man! Oh, if I were rich, I should know how to be generous too!

A dog, whose tail was nothing but a stump, came to sniff my fingers. I pushed it away, but it returned with such persistence that I blushed. I was sure my fingers did not smell.

Luckily the proprietress arrived, the necks of the bottles between her fingers and the bread under her arm. She kicked at the filthy animal and drove it away.

Billard prodded the Camembert with his fore-finger and cut it in two. He gave me half, the smaller one.

We ate slowly, on account of the cellophane paper which was sticking to the cheese.

When Billard drank, I copied him. Out of politeness I made sure that the level of my wine did not sink more quickly than his.

I am not accustomed to drink, so it was not long before I was tipsy. The broken-down old men who were chattering in a corner seemed like sages.

I poured out the rest of the wine and, as I expected, there was not much in my glass, because of the bump in the bottom of the bottle.

I leant back against a table. For the first time I looked my interlocutor in the eyes. He had finished eating too. He was picking his teeth with his tongue and making a hissing noise.

He was looking in his pockets for his tobacco. Without hesitation I offered him a cigarette.

I was in a mood to tell him the story of my life and, in a rush of candour, to tell him what I did not like about him.

'You seem to be a kind man, Monsieur Billard,' I said, and I noticed that the wine had altered my voice.

'Yes, I am kind.'

'There are so few people who understand life.'

'I am kind,' said Billard, who was pursuing his own train of thought. 'But you have to be careful, otherwise people take advantage of your generosity. It was on account of a friend that I lost my job.'

These words did not please me, and in order to find something we could agree about, I jumped from one subject to another.

'I was in the army.'

I took out my wallet and showed him my military passbook, with my name in big letters on the cover.

'I was in the army too,' he said, showing me his papers in return.

He unfolded them. He put his identity disc in my hand, and also a lock of hair flattened by its long stay in his wallet, a photograph showing him in service dress at one side of a piece of furniture, another showing him on fatigue next to a bucket, and another of a group of infantrymen in the middle of whom was a notice with these words on it: 'The lads of the 1st C.M. Why worry?'

'You see that one there?'

And he put his index finger on the head of one of the soldiers.

'Yes, I see him.'

'Well, he's dead too.'

I pretended to be interested in all this, but nothing bores me so much as other people's pocket-books and photographs with dirty backs. Besides, I saw so many of them during the war, so many pocket-books and photographs!

If I had not been drunk I should certainly not have displayed my papers. They must have bored Billard.

As he was searching in another envelope, I was afraid he was going to show me some naked women. I hate postcards like that. They just make me more wretched.

'I was at St. Mihiel,' I said, in order to speak about myself.

Instead of listening to me and asking questions:

'I was there too.'

'I was wounded and discharged.'

I showed him the splinter of shell which had wounded me.

'Do you live on your own?' asked Billard, folding his papers again.

'Yes.'

'You get fed up with it.'

'Oh, yes! — Especially in my case because I am so tender-hearted . . . Family life would have suited me. Look here, Monsieur Billard, if you would be my friend, I should be happy, really happy. I can't bear loneliness and poverty. I should like to have friends, to work, in short to be alive.'

'Have you got a mistress?'

'No.'

'But there's no shortage of women.'

'Yes . . . but I have no money. A mistress would bring me all sorts of worries. I should have to put on a clean shirt when I met her.'

'Oh come! You think women bother about what you wear. Of course, if you want to go around with a middle-class woman, that's different. Leave it to me; I'll find you a mistress. She will keep you amused.'

If he could indeed find me a woman, young and beautiful, who would love me and not bother about my clothes, why should I not accept?

'But it's difficult to find a pretty woman.'

'Not these days. Mine left all her boyfriends for me. I'm quite happy with that girl.'

I wanted an unhappy friend, a vagabond like myself, to whom I would be bound by no obligations. I had thought Billard was such a friend, poor and kind. I was mistaken. He kept on talking about his mistress — which plunged me into the deepest gloom.

'Bâton, come to my place tomorrow, after dinner, and you shall see the girl. I live in the rue Gît-le-Coeur, the Cantal Hotel.'

I accepted because I dared not refuse. I was quite sure I should never be brave enough to visit happy people.

Will my friendships always have to end in this ridiculous way?

We got up. In a mirror I had a view of myself up to the shoulders: I looked as if I were in court. Even though I was pretty drunk I recognized myself. However, the outline of my chest was fuzzy like someone's over-elongated shadow.

I crossed the room, followed by Billard.

Outside a rough wind like that at a railway-carriage window whipped me in the face. For a moment I thought of going with my companion, but I stopped myself: what use would it have been? For we were not really friends. Somebody loved him, he was well off and happy.

Besides, it was striking nine o'clock.

I should never have dared to say good-bye first; Billard was less considerate.

'See you tomorrow, Bâton.'

'Yes, see you tomorrow.'

I walked straight ahead until I should come to a familiar street.

The bars were warm, brightly lit and full of people. Although I was not thirsty, I was tormented by a longing to have something. I resisted at first, until it occurred to me that I had not thrown away any money that evening.

I went into the café.

Round the counter it was as steamy as a bathroom. A waiter was holding a glass up to the light.

I ordered what was cheapest: a black coffee.
'A large one?' asked the waiter.
'No, small.'

III

I spent the next day telling myself over and over again that I should not go to Billard's. He was quite capable of caressing his mistress in front of me. She would sit on his knee, she would tickle his ear.

These marks of affection would have riled me unbearably.

Lovers are rude and selfish.

Last year a young married couple lived in the dairy-woman's room. Every evening they used to settle themselves at the window, leaning on their elbows. From the sound of their kisses I could tell whether they were kissing on the mouth or not.

In order to avoid hearing them I used to linger in the streets until midnight. When I returned, I undressed in silence.

Once I had the misfortune to drop a shoe.

They woke up and the noise of their kisses began again. I knocked furiously on the wall. As I am not ill-disposed, I was sorry, a few moments later, that I had disturbed them. They must have been startled. I decided to apologize.

But, at nine o'clock in the morning, bursts of laughter could be heard through the wall. The two lovers were making fun of me.

In the evening after dinner I hung about in the boulevard Saint-Germain. The shops were no longer lit up. Arc-lamps illuminated the foliage of the trees. Long yellow trams glided along without wheels, like boxes. The restaurants were emptying.

The sound of eight o'clock striking rang through the air.

Although Billard was not the friend I dreamed of, I could not stop thinking about him.

My imagination invents perfect friends for the future, but, while I wait, I can make do with anyone at all.

It was possible that his mistress was not beautiful. I have noticed that one always imagines that women one does not know are beautiful. In the army, whenever a soldier talked to me about his sister, wife or cousin, I immediately used to picture a very handsome girl.

Not knowing how to pass the time, I turned in the direction of the Cantal Hotel. On the way, I was very much inclined to turn back, but the thought of an empty evening stretching ahead of me quickly got rid of this half-formed idea.

The rue Gît-le-Coeur smells of wine and foul water. The Seine runs close to its damp buildings. The children one meets are carrying bottles of wine. The passers-by walk in the road: there are no cars to worry about.

Here and there one of those lonely shops which close late sells cooked vegetables, green purées and potatoes steaming in zinc containers.

It was too early to go to Billard's. I do not like to take people by surprise, because they imagine that one is trying to find out what they are eating.

My overcoat was making my shoulders grow numb. A stitch in my side made me bend over as I walked. People feel sorry for you if you sit down on a bench in the evening.

I went into a bar on the place Saint-Michel and, as

usual, ordered a black coffee. I hung up my hat in a corner, opposite a mirror.

Some beautiful Egyptian women were filling their water-jugs on the ceramic walls. Two men in fashionable suits were playing chess. As I am not familiar with the rules of this game, the geometric movements of the pieces conveyed nothing to me.

The waiter, with his alpaca jacket cut away at the front, brought me my coffee. He was polite. He even brought me the *Illustration* in a folder.

I had scarcely opened this publication when the smell of the shiny paper reminded me that I was in a setting to which I was not accustomed. Nevertheless, I turned over the pages. In order to look at the photographs I had to lean forward because they reflected the light.

From time to time I glanced at my hat, to reassure myself that it was still there.

When I came to the advertisements, I closed the folder.

My saucer, which was full of cold coffee, had thirty centimes marked on it. I hoped this figure would be the price of the drink; but, as the saucers dated from before the war, I was afraid it might no longer be so.

'Waiter!'

It took him no more than a second to pick up my cup and wipe the table, even though I had not made it dirty.

'Thirty centimes, sir.'

I paid with a one franc piece. I was intending to give a tip of only two sous. At the last moment, afraid that it might not be enough, I left four sous.

I went out. My back did not hurt any more. The coffee still warmed my stomach.

I walked round the streets with the ease and satisfaction of an employee leaving his office. The im-

pression that I was playing a part in the crowd put me
in a good humour.

I put my last cigarette in my mouth, even though I
wanted to keep it for the following morning. Although
I had some matches, I preferred to ask a passer-by for a
light.

A man was standing on the strip of ground in the
middle of the street, smoking a cigar. I took care not to
approach him, because I know that cigar-smokers do
not like giving anyone a light: they attach great importance to the ash of their cigar.

Further on along my route — for I did have a route
— another man was smoking.

Raising my hat, I put my request to him. He held his
cigarette out to me and, so that it should not wobble,
rested his finger against my hand. His nails were well
cared for. He wore a signet-ring on his finger. His cuff
came down to his thumb.

Having thanked him three or four times, I went
away.

For a long time I thought about this unknown man. I
tried to guess what he thought of me and whether he
too was occupied with similar reflections.

One always hopes to make a good impression on
people one does not know.

IV

Above the door of the Cantal Hotel there was a white sphere with capital letters on it, like one of the globes at the Louvre.

I went in. Through a curtain I could make out a dining-room which must have been used as the office, a sideboard with rows of tiny balusters and a set of pigeon-holes in which letters were standing.

I knocked on the window-pane, very gently, in order not to break it. A curtain parted and a man tilted back his chair so he could see me.

'Can I help you?'

'Monsieur Billard, please.'

Without having to look it up, he replied:

'Thirty-nine, sixth floor.'

On the first floor the carpet stopped. Each door was numbered. Bundles of sheets cluttered up the staircase.

As I climbed the stairs I thought about Billard's mistress. To dispel the agitation which was getting hold of me, I kept on saying: she's ugly . . . she's ugly . . . she's ugly . . .

I reached the last floor quite out of breath. It seemed to me that my heart had moved from its place, it was beating so hard.

At last I knocked. The door was thin; it reverberated.

'Who's there?'

'Me.'

It would have been simpler to say my name, but because of my shyness I tried to avoid it. When I say my own name it always sounds very strange to me, especially behind a door.

'Who?'

I could no longer be silent.

'Bâton.'

Billard opened the door. I saw a woman sitting there and the whole room reflected in the mirror on the wardrobe door.

This girl was beautiful. Her curly hair twisted and coiled as if the lamp-light had burnt it.

Dumbfounded, I stayed on the threshold, on the point of running away.

She got up and came towards me.

Then an insane joy stopped me from speaking. The feeling that a warm breath was caressing my face made a shiver run over me. Although not normally given to high-spirited behaviour, I slapped Billard on the shoulder. In spite of my cheerfulness, I felt foolish as I withdrew my hand. I wanted to laugh, dance and sing: Billard's mistress had a limp.

The room was very ordinary. It could have been occupied by a Romanian, a prostitute or a clerk. The mantelpiece was cluttered up with newspapers on which saucepans had been put down, a toothbrush in a glass and some bottles.

'Nina, make some coffee!'

The girl lit a paraffin stove stained with egg-yolk.

This offer, because it meant I should have to stay, overwhelmed me with pleasure.

No doubt because he did not want to look as if he had noticed the silence which was becoming more embarrassing as time passed, Billard was looking for a nut in a box of tools and his mistress was cleaning the inside of some cups with her thumb. As for me, I wanted to speak, but everything I could think of would have made it too obvious that I was trying to put an end to a ludicrous situation.

When nobody was watching me, I looked round the room. The steam from the spout of the coffee-pot was spiralling upwards. The pillow-cases on the bed were grubby in the middle.

'Do you take milk?'

I replied that I did not mind.

We sat down round the table. Because I was afraid of brushing against my hosts' feet, I tucked my feet under my chair.

The speed with which the coffee had been made disconcerted me. I was well aware that I should have to go as soon as it had been drunk.

Nina poured out, holding on to the lid of the coffee-pot as she did so.

'I am sure your coffee is good,' I said, before I had tasted it.

'It comes from Damoy's.'

I stirred it for a long time, so that no sugar should be left at the bottom of the cup when I had drunk it. Then I swallowed with small mouthfuls, taking care not to upset anything as I raised the saucer to my mouth.

'More?' asked Nina.

Although my cup was small, I refused, out of politeness.

Suddenly, for no reason, Billard put his hand on mine.

My first thought was to pull mine away — I do not like being touched by men — but I did not do anything.

'Listen, Bâton.'

I looked at him. His nose was riddled with open pores.

'I have something to ask you.'

The prospect of being pleasant to a friend delighted me.

'Will you do something for me?'

'Yes . . . yes . . .'

I was afraid he would ask me something either too insignificant or too important. I like doing kindnesses, small kindnesses, of course, to demonstrate my goodwill.

'Lend me fifty francs.'

Our eyes met. A thousand thoughts rushed into my mind. Without a doubt it was the same with Billard. There was no longer any barrier between us. He could read me like a book, just as I could him.

The momentary hesitation which would afflict anyone in such a situation vanished and I said in a voice which I managed to make suitably solemn:

'I'll lend you them.'

I was happy, not so much because I was able to lend to him but because he was grateful to me. Conversation was picking up again. Now I was no longer embarrassed. I could stay until midnight and come back the next day and the day after and always. If he had borrowed fifty francs it was because he trusted me.

My pension money was in my pocket. Nevertheless I did not give Billard what he had asked. I gave the impression that I had forgotten about it. I felt that the longer I waited the longer he would go on being pleasant.

For the moment, I was acting a part. They kept their eyes on every movement, hoping that I would get out my wallet. I had not been so important for years. Every word of mine was greeted with a smile. They were watching me: they were afraid I might forget.

It would take a saint to resist the temptation of prolonging this pleasure.

Oh, I can easily forgive the rich!

It was beginning to get late. I stood up. Billard was pale: he did not dare repeat his request. I still pretended to have forgotten about it although I was thinking of nothing else.

Nina, with the lamp in her hand, and her head in the shadows, did not move.

Suddenly I had the impression that they had seen through my little game.

So, to deflect their suspicions, I pulled out my wallet with awkward hasty movements.

'How absent-minded I am . . . I was forgetting . . .'

I held out fifty francs.

'Thank you, Bâton, I'll pay you back next week.'

'Oh . . . there's no hurry!'

The gas-lights on the staircase had been put out. The mantles were still glowing like embers.

At that moment the two lovers must be looking at the bank-note against the light like a photographic plate, to satisfy themselves that it was good.

The feeling that I had had a trick played on me set me on edge. Billard had scarcely thanked me. He was not actually poor. He had a mistress, a cupboard full of linen, sugar, coffee and fat. He knew several people. Since this was so, why borrow money from a poor wretch like me? I had noticed several objects in his room. If he had taken them to the municipal pawn-office he could easily have got fifty francs.

I felt the carpet of the first-floor landing under my feet, then I saw, sitting in the dining-room, the proprietor reading a newspaper spread out at some distance from him.

Out in the street I shivered. The wind was blowing between the houses. A street-lamp stood in the middle of a circle of pale light.

I went a few steps with the brightness of the hotel

office in my eyes.

Raindrops were falling on the ground, never one on top of another.

V

That night I slept badly.

My covers kept falling off on one side of the bed. When the cold creeping up my legs aroused me, I stretched out a hand to find out where the wall was.

At dawn my window at last grew light. The table emerged slowly from the shadow, feet first. Squares appeared on the ceiling.

Suddenly it was day. The room was filled with clear light, as if the window-panes had been washed. I saw the motionless furniture, the ashes of some paper in the fire-place and the slats of the blind above the window.

The house stayed quiet for some minutes.

Then a door banged; the Lecoins' alarm-clock rang; a milk cart passed with the lids of the churns rattling.

I got up, for my bed was cold as it is when I sleep late.

People who have been sleeping between clean sheets can look at themselves in a mirror as soon as they jump out of bed. Before I look at myself in the morning, I have a wash.

Outside the sun was casting a golden light on the top storeys of the houses. It was not yet bright enough to dazzle the eyes.

The air which I drew in brought a mint-like freshness to my lungs.

A light wind, smelling of lilac, lifted the flaps of my overcoat, making it look like a military greatcoat.

There were no birds and no new buds; nevertheless it was spring.

I felt like walking. Usually when I leave home I go in the direction of the rue de la Seine. That day I decided to set out for the fortifications.

At the open windows underwear was hung out to dry and, stiffened by the wind, was swinging to and fro like metal sign-boards. Through the half-open doors of the shops newly washed floors could be seen, already dry.

The moment a seven-storey building hid the sun, I quickened my step.

The streets became dirtier and dirtier. Some buildings were shored up by beams among which children played when they came out of school. The earth showed through the broken surface of the pavements. The blackened plaster with which the buildings were faced looked like the studio background in photographs.

A cloud hid the sun. Warmth and colour left the street. Flies no longer glittered.

I felt sad.

A little while before I had set out for the unknown feeling like a vagabond, free and happy. Now, because of a cloud, everything was finished.

I retraced my steps.

In the afternoon, not knowing where to go, I hung about in the area round the Cantal Hotel.

It was in vain that I reasoned with myself. I told myself that if I met Billard we should not know what to say to each other, for it was impossible for me to go away from that district.

Perhaps those who live in poverty will understand this attraction.

Billard was of so little importance and yet he meant everything to me.

On the place Saint-Michel a man in a bowler hat was giving out hand-bills.

He gave me several.

People do not want to be bothered with these leaflets. They have to get their hands out of their pockets, take the papers, crumple them up and throw them away. What labour!

As for me, I am sorry for these distributors.

I always accept what they offer me. I know that these men are not free until after they have distributed several thousand pieces of paper.

People who pass contemptuously by these out-stretched hands instead of taking what they have to offer annoy me.

It was three o'clock. It is the time of day I dislike most. None of the little events of daily life cheers it up.

In order to put an end to my boredom I went back to the rue Gît-le-Coeur intending to call on Billard.

I passed in front of the door of the hotel four times, embarrassed at turning round. It is ridiculous to be embarrassed when one turns round in the street.

I did not go in.

I felt that Billard would not be glad to see me. On the day when he asked me for the fifty francs I ought to have given them immediately. He must certainly hold it against me that I made him wait.

However, I stayed there, at the corner of the street, keeping an eye on the hotel.

I had been looking at the windows of the houses for some minutes when Billard, accompanied by a man I did not know, appeared in the doorway.

I wanted to run to him, but as he would have

thought that I had been waiting for him for several hours, I stopped myself. He would never have been willing to admit that I had only just arrived.

People do not believe in chance, especially when it is that alone that can provide one with an excuse.

Billard had a new scarf. The hair at the back of his neck had been trimmed. The gestures he made as he spoke seemed to me those of a stranger. I have noticed that that is always the case when you catch sight of a friend with somebody you do not know and you yourself are unseen.

I hid behind a car. Billard would not be able to recognize me by my feet.

The two men were walking quickly in the middle of the road.

Then an odd and rather stupid idea came to me.

I turned into a parallel street and set off at the double. When I had covered a hundred metres I made my way along a street which crossed it back to the one I had just left.

Motionless in front of a shop, I waited.

To control the heaving of my chest, I breathed through my nose. My socks had fallen down over the uppers of my shoes.

The two men were approaching. To hear the clatter of their four feet you would have said that a horse was walking along the pavement.

In a few seconds Billard and his companion would be there.

I no longer dared to look at the shop window for fear that my eyes might meet those of Billard in the glass.

For a moment I thought of turning round with an absent-minded look. But I was afraid this absent-minded look might not seem natural.

Besides, Billard would see me. The street was narrow. He would imagine that I was just hanging about and would speak to me first.

That was what I wanted.

Unfortunately the two men passed me without a word.

The certainty that I had been seen prevented me from beginning the comedy over again.

I have no luck at all. Nobody takes any interest in me. People treat me as if I were cracked. Nevertheless I am kind and generous too.

Henri Billard was a scoundrel. He would never repay my fifty francs. That is how the world always rewards you.

I was angry and miserable. The feeling that my whole life would elapse in loneliness and poverty increased my despair.

It was hardly four o'clock. I should have to wait for at least two hours before going to a restaurant.

Transparent clouds were hurrying along below other black clouds. The streets were losing the tiring atmosphere of the afternoon, no doubt because of the appearance of the evening papers.

I have noticed that these papers arouse the passers-by, even those who do not buy them. A newspaper is made to be read in the morning. When it appears in the evening it seems that it must have some important reason for doing so.

Billard had offended me deeply. All the same I could not bring myself to leave his neighbourhood.

I walked quickly along the streets where I thought I had been noticed, slowly along those where I was going for the first time.

A woman with a limp made me think of Nina. It was impossible that she should love Billard. She was too young. A girl of eighteen does not live with a man of forty unless she is forced to.

Little by little the idea of going to see Nina in-sinuated itself into my mind.

I felt brave enough. When I am alone with a woman my shyness does not bother me. I rather have the impression it makes her like me.

Yes, I should know how to talk to that girl. I should revile Billard to her. She would understand. She would leave him. And, who knows? Perhaps she would love me!

At the sight of the Cantal Hotel's white globe I had the feeling that, in order not to wake in the middle of a wonderful dream, I was forcing myself to sleep.

I entered the hotel, trying to persuade myself that I had come directly from home, that I was late, that after all there was nothing in the least odd about my visit.

I climbed the stairs slowly, so I should not get out of breath. My hands, wet with sweat, squeaked on the banister.

A maid with her hair tied up in a duster was sweep-ing a dark corridor. Through an open window I saw a courtyard and the back of a house where some meat-safes were hung up like bird-cages.

In the middle of the last flight I stopped.

If a door had opened I should have continued on my way. I did not wish to appear to be a shady character as people do when they hang about on landings.

I was extremely agitated. My ears were humming as if I were listening to the sound of the sea in a shell. My shirt was wet under the arms.

Having ascended the last few steps I knocked.

'Who's there?'

'Bâton . . . Bâton.'

'Oh! right . . . wait . . . I'm washing.'

Stuck in front of the door like a man from the gas

company, I listened for the tiniest noise, afraid of
hearing the voice of Billard or a stranger.

Light was coming through the keyhole. Anyone else
would have looked. I did not. It is true I should have
died of shame if anyone had surprised me crouching at
the door.

Nina appeared at last.

Freshly washed, with her hair wet round the temples,
her eyelashes stuck together, darker than usual, her lips
moist, without a wrinkle, she was smiling. She had
lovely teeth: you could not see her gums.

'Come in, Monsieur Bâton.'

'I'm disturbing you.'

'No.'

She ought to have repeated her denial several times.

She walked ahead of me, not embarrassed by her
limp.

When she stopped, she held her body upright again.

'Is Monsieur Billard here?'

'He has just gone out.'

'That's a pity.'

'Wait for him, then.'

I settled myself in the same place as the day before. It
is a habit of mine. I always sit in the place I chose the
first time.

The room no longer had the air of cleanliness which
a polished floor, a wardrobe with a mirror and a black
marble fireplace give by lamplight.

Bits of gleaming wood were coming loose from the
furniture. The wallpaper looked as if it had been dried
in the sun. The air smelt of toothpaste. There were
machine-embroidered flowers on the curtains. The
casters of the bed had made lines on the wooden floor.

'Don't turn round, Monsieur Bâton, I must finish
getting dressed.'

This word dress made me want to seize the girl by

the waist, no doubt because it made me think of un-
dressing.

I was afraid Billard would arrive. What on earth
would he have said if he had found me there while his
mistress was putting on her clothes! He would have
been jealous.

I could hear the little noise of the press-studs, the
crackling of a clean blouse being unfolded and from
time to time the cracking of a joint.

My eyes hurt from squinting so hard at the girl.

When she had finished dressing she came and sat
down opposite me.

Even though it was unnecessary I turned: it was an
instinctive movement.

I saw a pair of knickers with the legs touching at just
one point and, on the floor, the prints of a foot, with
five toes.

'How are you, Monsieur Bâton?'

'Fairly well . . . and you?'

She did not reply. Without bothering about me, she
was filing her nails.

As I imagined that once her nails had been filed she
would take an interest in me, I counted the fingers
which had not yet been attended to.

She put down her whitened file.

'You must get bored when Henri is away?'

'Yes, a bit.'

She pulled down her skirt to hide her stunted leg.

'You must be happy with him.'

'Yes.'

As Nina's reply seemed decidedly lacking in en-
thusiasm, I murmured.

'I understand.'

She looked closely at me. Her hands stopped
moving.

'I understand,' I repeated. 'He bores you.'

'Who?'

'Billard.'

There was a silence. She was motionless. Only her eyes moved. Both at once.

Now I was quite sure she did not care for her lover. She was too ill at ease when I spoke of him. She did not defend him.

I got up. For the first conversation it would be better not to rush things.

As she was showing me out, she gave me her hand quite frankly, without bending her elbow.

Since we were alone, I kept her hand in mine.

I found myself on the landing. She was standing in the doorway. She was looking at my ears to see if I were blushing.

'Good-bye.'

'Good-bye.'

I had just a second left to arrange a meeting before she closed the door.

'Tomorrow, at three o'clock,' I mumbled.

She did not reply.

Without looking at the steps, a bit like a fairy, I flew down the stairs.

VI

A few seconds later I was outside, red to the collar; I was short of breath as if it were windy.

I looked at my reflection in a window. A vein I did not know I had ran across my forehead from top to bottom.

I should gladly have gone back to the hotel and kissed Nina. She liked me. It took somebody as shy as I was not to know how to take advantage of the situation. No doubt she regretted that I had not been more enterprising. My feebleness must have annoyed her.

But if she were intelligent she would be grateful to me for having respected her. It is improper to kiss a person one hardly knows.

I was about to have a mistress who would love me and who, in return for giving herself to me, would ask for nothing.

In order that the night should seem less long, I went home late.

When I had taken off my jacket, I leaned on my elbows at the window. The mild air reminded me of the evenings of the previous summer. The moon, covered with watery stains, lit up the edge of a cloud.

Then I went to bed.

I had to sleep, otherwise I should not have looked good in the morning.

My face is not symmetrical. My jaw is more prominent on the left. When I am tired this becomes more obvious.

Nevertheless I could not manage to close my eyes. It was in vain that I kept on remaking my bed, that I stood naked at the window to cool myself, I still thought about Nina. I saw her before me, mistily, like a picture on a postcard, without legs, or else I tried to think of a way of getting her to my room without the concierge's noticing.

As I still could not get to sleep, I decided to review in my imagination all the incidents of my life in the army. It is odd that, in the memory, places where one has been unhappy become pleasant.

Just as I hardly ever sing the songs of my childhood in order not to blunt the memories they evoke, so I only think about my life as a soldier when I cannot do anything else. I like to keep a store of memories in my mind. I know it is there. It is enough for me.

I was becoming drowsy when the woman from the dairy, who was no doubt coming back from the cinema, banged her door.

She closed her window, then she washed. She never washed herself in the evening. I could hear the same noises as I had outside Billard's door. I have noticed that new experiences in everyday life often come in groups.

I got out of bed.

With my toes in the air because of the cold, I roamed about the room, vaguely hoping that the woman from the dairy would see me through some hole in the wall.

It was already dawn when I fell asleep. I did not hear the Lecoins' alarm clock, nor the sweeping of the concierge who, every morning, bumps into my door on purpose.

When I woke up, the square of sunlight had gone past my bed and was trembling on the wall.

It was late. I got up in a hurry, with my eyes half-closed and one cheek striped like a leaf by a crumpled sheet.

As soon as I was dressed I brushed my clothes thoroughly.

My brush is so old that the bristles stick in the fabric.

I have to pick them out one by one.

Then I went out.

It was a beautiful spring day. The sun was overhead. I was walking on my shadow.

I own a safety-razor. But the blade is blunt.

That is why I went into a barber's shop.

The proprietor was sweeping up hair. He was in his shirt-sleeves. He wore nickel-plated arm-bands above the elbows. His tie was held in place by a clip.

He shaved me very well.

At exactly three o'clock, with my skin taut and my face powdered, I knocked at Billard's door.

Nina must be waiting for me.

The veins in my hands were bigger than usual.

Nobody answered. Nina, who was a tease, must be trying to keep me on tenter-hooks.

I knocked, more loudly this time.

With my ear glued to the door, I listened. You can hear better like that.

Not a sound broke the silence.

Then I banged with my fist. The same silence. Nina was not there. I looked through the keyhole, because there was nobody about. I could see half the window with a curtain that was too long.

Nina had not waited for me; Nina did not love me.

Suddenly, I was seized with senseless terror. If the girl were dead, there in the room, I should be suspected.

I rushed down the stairs, jumping the last two steps of each floor.

That is how my involvement with the Billard pair

came to an end. I have not gone back to see them even to ask for my fifty francs.

I avoid the place Saint-Michel. However, if Billard had wanted to, we could have been so happy.

I am looking for a friend. I do not think I shall ever find one.

Neveu the Bargeman

I like wandering about beside the Seine. The docks, the basins, the sluice-gates make me think of some distant port where I should like to live. In my imagination I see sailors and girls dancing together, little flags, motionless ships with sails furled.

These thoughts do not last.

I know the wharves of Paris too well: only for a moment do they look like the misty cities of my dreams.

One afternoon in March I was walking along the embankment. It was five o'clock. The wind blew out my overcoat like a skirt and I had to hold on to my hat. From time to time a passenger steamer with its glassed-in windows passed by on the water, moving more quickly than the current. The bark of the trees glistened with moisture. Without turning round it was possible to see the tower of the Gare de Lyon, with its clock-faces already lit up. When the wind dropped, the air smelled of dried-up gutters.

I stopped and, leaning on the parapet, gazed miserably before me.

The funnels of the tugs were tilted backwards as they approached the bridges. Some barges with people living on them were tied up by taut cables in the middle of the river. A long gangplank reached from a lighter to the bank. The workman who was venturing out on it bounced with every step, as if he were on a sprung mattress.

I had no intention of dying, but I have often wanted to arouse pity. As soon as a passer-by approached I hid my face in my hands and sniffed like someone who has been crying. People turned as they went past me.

Last week I came within a hair's breadth of throwing myself into the water in order to make it appear I was in earnest.

I was gazing at the river, thinking of the Gaulish coins there must be on the bottom, when a tap on my shoulder made me jerk up my elbow, quite instinctively.

I turned round, embarrassed at having been frightened.

There facing me was a man in a sailor hat, with the fag-end of a cigarette protruding from his moustache and an identity disc rusting on his wrist.

As I had not heard him coming, I looked at his feet. He was wearing rope-soled shoes.

'I know you want to die,' he said.

I did not reply: silence made me interesting.

'I know I'm right.'

I opened my eyes as wide as I possibly could, to make them water.

'Yes, I know.'

Since my eyes would not water, I closed them. There was a silence, then I murmured:

'That's right, I want to die.'

Night was falling. The street-lamps were coming on. Only one part of the sky was still light.

The stranger approached and spoke into my ear:

'I want to die too.'

At first I thought he was joking: but, as his hands

were trembling, I was suddenly afraid that he might
mean it and that he might invite me to die with him.

'Yes, I want to die,' he repeated.

'Oh, come on!'

'I want to die.'

'You must hope in the future.'

I like the words 'hope' and 'future' in the silence of
my head, but as soon as I speak them it seems to me
that they lose their meaning.

I thought the bargeman would burst out laughing.
He did not stir.

'You must hope.'

'No . . . No . . .'

I began to talk without stopping in order to dissuade
him from dying.

He did not listen to me. With his body upright, his
head lowered and his arms hanging at his sides, he
looked like a ruined banker.

Fortunately he seemed to have forgotten that I too
had been thinking of killing myself. I took care not to
remind him of it.

'Let's go,' I said, hoping to get away from the river-
side.

'Yes, let's go down to the edge.'

A little while before the stone of the parapet had
chilled my elbows. Now the cold was getting a hold on
my body.

'Down to the edge?' I asked.

'Yes . . . we must die.'

'It's too dark at the moment. We'll come back tomorrow.'

'No, today.'

It would have been cowardly to run away. I should
have had it on my conscience for the rest of my life. It is
not right to let anyone die. My duty was to save this
man. But, while he stayed there, he imagined that I

wanted to drown myself and if I refused at the last
minute he was quite capable of compelling me to it.
Bargemen are used to pulling boats along at the end of
a rope. It must be easy for them to drag a man by the
arm.

'It would be better to go home, my friend.'

The man raised his head. He was wearing an English
military tunic with no buttons. No doubt he had given
them away. Under this tunic, he had a sweater, slack at
the neck, which was bunched up over his stomach. His
teeth were badly overcrowded. A few coarse hairs
protruded from his ears. A bottle of wine with a new
cork was sticking half-way out of his pocket.

He took me by the arm and dragged me towards a
small staircase. When I looked down I could see the
bank between the iron steps.

I went down slowly, putting both feet on each step
before going on, like somebody with a wooden leg.

I held on to the narrow, flat hand-rail and, to delay
the suicide, I pretended to be afraid of falling.

The bargeman dug his fingers in between the
muscles and the bone. From time to time I raised my
arm to try to free myself: it was no good.

On the bank were a pointed heap of sand, some tools
belonging to the city of Paris, a hut and a chained-up
wheelbarrow. I could see the dark underside of a
bridge and the tops of the buses passing along the
embankment. Gusts of wind struck me in the back.

'It's easier to die when there are two of you,' com-
mented my companion.

There was no doubt that this bargeman had decided
to drown himself. He thought I would follow him. I
wanted him to go on thinking that. It is not pleasant
when people suspect you of being afraid of death.

We were on the edge of the Seine as if we were on the
edge of a pond. There was no parapet here. I was

astonished to find myself so close to the river. To see
the Seine flowing between the houses under the stone
bridges, who would have thought it possible to get so
near it?

In spite of myself I remembered, as I always do
when I see an expanse of water, that I could not swim.

'Let's go a bit further,' said the stranger. 'The
current will carry us against the arches of this bridge.'

I agreed at once.

A tram made the crown of the bridge tremble.
Every time I pass beneath a bridge I am gripped by the
same fear. The gravel crunched beneath our feet like
powdered sugar.

'But why are you so determined to die?' I asked.

'I haven't eaten for three days. I don't know where
to sleep.'

'There are refuges.'

'I'm too well known there. They don't want me any
more.'

Reflections ran straight down into the Seine. The
surface of the river stirred as if there were seals beneath
the water. On the other side, because of the shadow,
the houses looked as if they went right down to the
river, as they do in Venice.

'Come on; be brave,' said the bargeman. 'There's
just one bad minute to get through. After that, ever-
lasting rest.'

'Are you sure?'

'Yes . . . come on . . . be brave.'

His hand, which was still gripping me in the same
place, provoked the same fear as an unseen crab
pinching the foot.

'Let go of me first.'

I did not want to kill myself, but even if I had
decided to I should not have wanted anyone to hold on
to me. One needs all one's independence to kill oneself.

Suicide is not the same as death.

Contrary to what I was expecting, the stranger let go immediately.

Air poured into my lungs as if, instead of releasing my arm, he had let go of my throat.

The bargeman stooped, and with two fingers tested the temperature of the water.

'A bit cold,' he said, wiping his hand.

'So we had better come back another time.'

'No, we must get it over with.'

All through my life I have found myself in situations like that. It is because of my loneliness. I want people to be interested in me and like me. As I do not know anyone, I try to attract attention in the street, because that is the only place where anyone could notice me.

My case is like that of a beggar singing on a bridge in the middle of winter at midnight. The passers-by do not give him anything because they find that way of asking for charity is a bit too theatrical. In the same way when they see me leaning on a parapet, miserable and with nothing to do, passers-by guess I am acting a part. They are right. All the same, do you not think it very sad to be reduced to begging on a bridge at midnight or to leaning on a parapet to arouse people's interest?

The bargeman was filling his pockets with stones in order to sink more quickly.

'Do what I'm doing,' he said.

The situation was getting worse. I did not really want to mention my money, but now I could be silent no longer. Right up to the last moment I had been hoping that some unforeseen event would spare me the necessity of saying that I had a little money.

'Well, well . . .'

The man, who was crouching by a heap of sand and picking out the stones, turned round.

'We're saved!'

He looked at me uncomprehendingly.

'I've just noticed that I have a little money.'

The stranger stood up and took a step forward. Some pebbles slipped from his fingers. His eyes glittered, just in the middle.

'You have got some money?'

'Yes . . . yes.'

'Show me, show me.'

I opened my wallet. So that he should not see all my notes, I pulled out just one which unfolded as it emerged.

'Here you are. Take this ten-franc note.'

The wretched man looked at the note lovingly and, for a whole minute, he endeavoured to get the creases out of it.

We went into a restaurant and I led the way.

'What will you have?'

I now addressed him familiarly, because he owed me his life and also because he was poorer than I.

'The same as you.'

'Some red, then?'

'Yes.'

We were brought some wine in a newly-washed bottle, a split loaf and four sausages which sizzled on our plates.

I paid.

I always pay in advance. In this way my mind is at rest. I know that the money left in my purse is entirely my own.

The bargeman threw himself on to the sausages.

'Be careful, eat slowly.'

He did not answer. I felt then that I was becoming less important in his eyes.

When he had finished, I asked:

'Have you had a good meal?'

He wiped his moustache with the palm of his hand before replying, 'Yes.'

I was annoyed that he did not show more sign of gratitude.

To remind him of the present I had made him, I asked:

'Have you still got the ten francs?'

'Yes.'

He certainly had no tact. In his place I should have been much more polite to a benefactor. Luckily for him he was dealing with me. I am broad-minded and charitable. Ingratitude does not prevent me from doing good.

'What is your name?'

'Neveu . . . and yours?'

Now he was addressing me familiarly. I have noticed that it is better not to be familiar with badly brought up people. They confuse familiarity with friendship. They immediately assume that they are your equal. The gap which separates you disappears. Besides, I myself have never been familiar with anyone who, being my superior, would treat me familiarly. I know only too well how that annoys people.

I bore Neveu no grudge, but he ought to have been more tactful. I certainly had been with Billard.

Since I am very kind, I answered my neighbour:

'Victor Bâton.'

Now his cheeks over the bone were red like ripe fruit. His beard was curlier. There were crumbs of bread sticking to his sweater.

Neveu, in spite of his lack of good manners, seemed to me a likeable person. At last I had found a friend I could count on. He would know no one but me. I should have no occasion for jealousy. Besides, I was proud of being more resourceful than he was. When we went out together, he would go along the streets that I liked; he would stop in front of my favourite shops.

'Where are you sleeping tonight?' I asked, knowing very well he had nowhere to live.

'I don't know.'

'Don't worry, I'll look after you.'

My first thought was to make up a bed for him in my room. But I quickly abandoned that idea. First, the concierge would have been furious with me. Then, my bed is a sacred thing. Like everybody else I am a creature of habit, especially in my bedroom. If I had to sleep with one blanket less than usual, I should not have slept a wink all night. In the morning I should have been embarrassed to wash myself. It would be better for me to rent him a small room at an hotel. For ten francs a week it would be possible to find a reasonably good attic.

Having come to this conclusion, I gave the matter no further thought. However, I took good care not to tell the bargeman. I preferred to leave him wondering.

At that moment I felt that I was once again his good angel. He was pale. When rich people are upset they know how to conceal it. He was poor and he did not know how to do that. His hands twitched like those of people who are asleep when a fly walks over them. His eyes moved as sharply as a negro's.

It is not very good to take pleasure in having someone at one's mercy. However, I had an excuse, because, if I was keeping him on tenter-hooks, it was only so that I could give him some good news a little while later. I should not have behaved in this way if I had not been willing to take care of him.

'Do you want a drink, my friend?'

'Yes.'

I ordered another bottle of wine.

As we clinked glasses I noticed that my nails were

cleaner than those of my companion. I did not know if I ought to be pleased or embarrassed.

As soon as the glasses were empty I poured out some more for fear that Neveu would get in before me. If he had taken the liberty of serving me I should have been shocked. It would have seemed to me that he was taking no account of my superiority. He already addressed me familiarly: it was quite enough.

We were in good spirits. My head was spinning, as if I were on a swing. I felt myself becoming kind, without reservation, really kind.

'You don't need to worry about anything, you know, Neveu, I'll rent a room for you. If you want, we can be real friends. We'll never leave each other.'

The bargeman's expression changed suddenly, perhaps because of a lock of hair which fell over his temple. The wrinkles which ran from his nostrils to the corners of his mouth became less deep.

'Yes . . . yes . . . if you want.'

The familiar way in which he addressed me shocked me, but less than the first time, all the same. I realized that I had been wrong. Drunkenness made me want to share everything I had.

'Come on, let's go,' I said, giving the skirts of my overcoat, which were sprinkled with sawdust, a shake.

In spite of my state I was well aware that the last bottle of wine had not been paid for. I pretended to have forgotten.

Neveu, in order not to remind me, took out the note I had given him.

'How much?' he asked the woman.

I had unconsciously been waiting for this question to break in.

'No . . . no . . . leave it . . . I'll pay.'

The cool outdoor air did not get rid of my drunkenness. The street, which was full of people, was blurry,

as it is when one tries on someone else's spectacles.
People's heads looked like masks. The car headlights
went by at the level of my stomach. I had cottonwool
in my ears. The motors of the taxis seemed like so
much hot scrap iron, quite without value. The pavement wobbled beneath my feet, like a weighing-
machine. It seemed like a street in a dream, with lights
scattered haphazardly.

I was so happy I wanted to shout it out aloud.

Now I no longer wished to share with Neveu: I
wanted to give him everything. I felt that my poverty
was not great enough. Great Heavens, what joy is
more lofty than that of giving away everything one has
and then, with empty hands, watching the person who
has been made happy.

I was going to offer Neveu everything when a
sudden thought stopped me. Perhaps he was not
worthy.

We had been walking for five minutes when an idea
such as might well come from a well-fed man occurred
to me:

'I say . . . let's go to Flora's!'

'Flora's?'

'It's a place where people can have a good time.'

The bargeman, who was drunk, was walking askew,
with one shoulder lower than the other. He was following the edge of the pavement like a tightrope-
walker. With his elbow on his stomach and his hand
trembling at the level of his chin, he looked as if he had
completely gone to pieces. His head wobbled like a
balloon held by a short string. One end of the cord
round his waist hung down to his knees.

'You see, Neveu, it's better here than under the
water.'

I had never been so happy. My friend was following

me. So I was leading him. I thought that it would not have mattered whether I turned left or right, because the bargeman would have followed me.

In spite of the throng the path before us was always clear. When we had to cross the road, as if by chance a policeman held up the traffic. When a crowd blocked the pavement, a way through appeared just as we got there.

We went along the empty street. The light of the street-lamps wavered over the houses, up to the first floor. Our shadows, cut short at the knee, sometimes went before us and sometimes followed us on the walls. A brightly-lit window high up in a house threw its square of light, enlarged and dim, on to the front of the building opposite.

For a time I leaned against a wall: the plaster got under my nails.

Or else I fingered my inside pocket, for in spite of my drunkenness I had my mind on my wallet. I was afraid my neighbour might take advantage of my condition and steal it.

A gramophone blared out. A door was lit up by a number.

We had arrived.

I ought to say that I should never have dared go there alone. It is not the same when there are two of you. People's attention is not focused on you alone.

Nevertheless, nervousness made my stomach ache.

So I was about to enter one of these establishments which I had heard about from childhood. And I was about to enter as a leader and not just one of a troop, as if I were in the army.

I rang the bell.

No doubt in order to protect us from the unpleasantness of being seen standing there, the door opened straightaway.

We went in.

The door was fitted with a special gadget and closed all by itself.

Immediately I remembered my hat. I took it off and, in order to seem like a regular customer, I walked straight ahead.

'Not that way!' shouted a big woman, the one who had opened the door.

She had white stockings, a leather bag on a steel chain and a lace apron, too small to be any use as an apron.

I stopped. This reprimand had spoiled my entrance. I so much wanted to seem to be familiar with these places.

She showed us into a room which surprised us by its size, like all rooms which lie in the depths of a house.

A few customers, who did not mind being bored, were watching the gramophone record going round. At the end of the room there was an empty stage with some motley scenery.

'The young ladies are eating. They will be down in a few minutes. What will you have while you wait, gentlemen?'

I know that drinks are very expensive in these places. Nevertheless I ordered a bottle of wine.

We sat down.

I had kept my overcoat on because it is very difficult to get into it because of the sleeve lining.

Neveu's behaviour annoyed me. He had not taken off his cap. Besides, he had no collar. And instead of showing the humility suitable to his poverty he was behaving in a very tiresome way.

I nudged him with my elbow.

'Take your cap off.'

He obeyed. A red line from temple to temple divided his forehead.

While my companion rubbed his eyes with a wet forefinger, I cleaned my nails with a match, under the table.

Some of the lamps had not yet been lit. It felt like being in a cinema when one has arrived too early. The customers looked as if they had been compelled to be there. Their hands were in their pockets. Their red ears shone like their noses. The imitation leather of the seats gleamed like worn-out silk serge.

The gramophone stopped.

A customer mimicked the sound. It cannot be difficult because I have known lots of people who could do that.

At last the women appeared. I counted them. There were seven of them.

Their short skirts emitted the same odour of vice and wretchedness as the spangled dresses in which the wax monsters exhibited in travelling shows are decked out.

Their skin was pale and gleaming like dolls made of glazed cardboard. Rings sparkled in rows on their fingers.

When one of the prostitutes was alone, her legs seemed well-shaped, but as soon as she joined her companions their faults leapt into prominence, though I could not tell why that was.

A woman came and sat down near us and bounced up and down on the seat as she laughed. She had yellow teeth which, because of the whiteness of her face, seemed even more yellow. The whites of her eyes were lined like an old clock-face. The scent she gave out smelled stronger when she moved.

Neveu looked at her admiringly. He had changed completely. He was talking and laughing and no longer paying any attention to me.

Suddenly the woman got up and, taking the bargeman by the arm, drew him away.

I was left alone. On the table were three glasses and two bottles.

I paid for the lot and went out, with my soul full of bitterness.

I was ready to do anything for Neveu. I liked him, weaker than I as he was.

I gave him ten francs: instead of keeping them to buy food, he preferred to amuse himself. Today, he is perhaps dead, drowned. Nevertheless, if he had listened to me, if he had liked me, if he had not made fun of me, we should have been happy.

On that day I too should have been glad to go with a woman. I did not do so because I wanted to rent a room for him.

He did not guess what depths of tenderness lay within me. He preferred to satisfy a desire.

If you do good, that's all the thanks you will get.

Is it really so difficult to come to an understanding in this life?

Monsieur Lacaze

I

Stations give me a glimpse of a world with which I am not familiar. The atmosphere which surrounds them is exceptionally pervasive.

I like stations, particularly the Gare de Lyon. The square tower which dominates it reminds me, no doubt because it is new, of the public buildings in German cities at which I gazed from the doorways of cattle-trucks when I was a soldier.

I like stations because they are alive day and night. If I cannot sleep I feel less alone.

Stations disclose the private life of rich people. In the street they look like everyone else. When they are leaving Paris, I hear them talking, laughing and giving orders. I see how they part. All this fascinates me, because I am poor, without friends, without luggage.

It is most unlikely that these travellers would wish to change places with anyone who, like me, was watching them leave.

Tall young women wait while their trunks are registered. They are beautiful. I scrutinize them wondering whether, if they were dressed in working clothes, they would look as lovely.

I like the Gare de Lyon because, behind it, is the Seine with its steep banks, its cranes turning in the air, its motionless barges like small islands and its columns of smoke hanging in the sky, where they have ceased to climb.

One day, not knowing how to occupy my time, I decided to spend a few hours in the Gare de Lyon.

The swing-doors beat against the air. My feet slipped on the glazed tile floors, as they would in a pine forest. Magazines were sticking to the damp window-panes of a kiosk. It was so draughty that people could not open their newspapers. Although it was daylight the lights were on in the ticket office. The railway officials seemed to be rather like policemen.

Nobody paid any attention to me. I was miserable. I made myself stay there. I wanted the travellers to feel a twinge of remorse as they left, to spare a thought for me as they travelled to other lands.

I walked with my head lowered and when I met a pretty woman I looked sadly at her in order to arouse her pity. I hoped she would guess how much I needed love.

Whenever I leave my house, I expect something to happen which will change my whole life. I wait for it until I go home again. That is why I never stay in my room.

Unfortunately nothing has ever happened.

'Hey . . . you over there!'

Turning round I saw, twenty metres away, a man who must have been standing in a draught: his overcoat billowed out as if he had been on the bridge of a ship. A case dangled from his right arm.

Not knowing whether he was addressing me, I waited. Then he beckoned with his forefinger, as if he were pulling a trigger.

I looked round to make sure he was not summoning anyone else and, seeing nobody, I approached.

The stranger was fat. His stomach protruded from

his jacket. The bristles of his ginger moustache were cut evenly.

I was annoyed, not because he took me for a porter, but because he was disturbing my bitter sorrow. Someone was actually talking to me now! I was like everyone else. Because of this man I no longer had the right to complain.

'Take this case, my man.'

He was lazy as people are who have travelled and who find it quite natural that others should rush towards them and clear a way for them.

I hesitated to take the case: a girl was watching us.

At last, having decided to submit, I seized the handle with my good hand and followed the traveller.

His overcoat was up at the back, no doubt because he had been sitting on it.

I kept on stopping to rest and look at my crushed fingers.

As for the traveller, he did not stop when I did. He went on his way and waited farther on, so that he did not have to speak to me.

I kept my eyes lowered all the way because I was ashamed. The case was rubbing against my leg and making my trousers slip.

I wanted to tell this man the story of my life: perhaps he would take an interest in me. I attached all the more importance to it in that, if I had not done it, I should have been angry with myself.

At certain times it was easy to tell people about my unhappiness, at others it was impossible, especially when I was getting ready to speak.

For every time I braced myself to speak, the traveller was looking for something in his pocket or gazing attentively into the distance. It did not need anything more to put me off. I was afraid of bothering such an important man. I felt that, if he were to listen to me, it was essential that he should have nothing else to do.

As soon as were were out on the pavement a taxi drew up in front of us.

I found the door as difficult to open as if it had been the door of a railway carriage: I did not know which way the handle turned.

The driver lowered his flag and looked us up and down, like a horseman.

He was so composed that I knew my efforts to pick up the case must seem absurd to him.

The gentleman gave his address fairly loudly, because of the engine, then sorting through some change in his hand he picked out a coin and held it out to me.

I felt that in a second or two I should blush. Not so much out of pride but rather to make myself interesting, I refused. I even made a gesture of refusal with my hand.

'Don't you want it?' enquired the traveller in a changed tone, addressing me less familiarly.

This refusal, although it was ordinary enough, had made an impression on him.

The driver, purple as a varicose vein, was watching us, with his hands on the steering wheel.

'Why refuse? You're poor.'

At that moment I ought to have stammered something and got away. But I stayed, hoping for I know not what.

'You interest me, my man.'

The stranger took out a visiting card and, resting it on the taxi, he wrote: 'Ten o'clock.'

'Here you are . . . come and see me tomorrow morning.'

He climbed into the car, which rocked like a boat.

Motionless, with the card in my hand, not knowing what to say and wanting to say something, I stayed there on the edge of the pavement.

The taxi turned round in the courtyard and passed in front of me again. The driver looked at me as much as to say: 'Push off, you scoundrel!' For a second I glimpsed the gentleman who was lighting a cigarette.

The taxi went away. Without knowing why, I took its number.

I did not want anyone to see me reading the card. As people were watching me, I moved away.

It was only after I had been walking for five minutes that I read:

JEAN-PIERRE LACAZE
Manufacturer
6, rue Lord-Byron

This card made a great impression on me, because of the double-barrelled Christian name, the word 'manufacturer' and because of the rue Lord-Byron, which was certainly not in my part of the city.

Yes, the next day I should go to see the gentleman, at ten o'clock.

So I was saved, because someone was taking an interest in me.

II

When I got home in the evening, I washed my socks and handkerchief in my basin, in cold water.

That night I woke up every quarter of an hour, before the end of a dream on each occasion. Then I thought about the manufacturer. In my imagination he had a daughter whom I married; he died bequeathing his fortune to me.

In the morning, when I opened my eyes, I realized that my imagination had led me too far. Monsieur Lacaze was probably no different from other men.

While I was getting ready, I went over the events in my life which might possibly interest him, so that I could tell him about them.

Then I made my choice. One may well be unhappy, poor and alone, but there are always things about which it is better to say nothing.

I have two suits: the one I wear every day and another which has the advantage of being black. I hesitated to put on the latter; I did not know whether Monsieur Lacaze would prefer me to look poor or whether he would be glad I had dressed my best for him.

I decided to put on the black suit. I brushed the stains, having spat on the brush. I have been brushing these stains for a long while. They always reappear in the evening.

I washed my arms right up to the elbows so no one

would notice my body was dirty. I dampened my hair so that my parting would stay in place. I put on a clean shirt, the only stiff collar I have (it had only been worn twice) and the least crumpled of my ties.

I went out.

I did not put on my hat immediately so that my hair had time to dry. I have noticed that there is nothing uglier than hair which has dried beneath a hat.

I had my pocket-book with all my papers with me. Monsieur Lacaze's card was in an empty pocket, so that I should not have to hunt for it if I needed it.

It was eight o'clock. It was unusual for me to go down so early. The stairs had not yet been swept. There was a newspaper straddling the doctor's door knob.

The doctor is an excellent man, like all educated people.

At nine o'clock I was already walking in the area of the Champs Elysées.

To see the houses and trees emerging from a yellow fog reminded one of a photograph which had not been fixed. Nevertheless one felt that the sun would get through at midday.

I asked a policeman where the rue Lord-Byron was.

With his arm stretched out under his cape, he showed me.

I listened, wondering what he would think if I went straight off in a different direction.

The house in the rue Lord-Byron which displays the number 6 is wealthy. That is immediately obvious. The ground floor windows are of stained glass. The metal shutters fold like a screen. Above the main entrance two masks are carved in the stone: tragedy and comedy, no doubt. The drive is edged with two small footpaths, so that people can be safe when a car is coming out.

A well-dressed concierge was sweeping the pavement which was already clean. He noticed me. This annoyed me because he would recognize me a few minutes later when I came back.

I was crossing the street in order to get a view of the whole house when, being suddenly afraid that Monsieur Lacaze might see me, I quickened my pace with the absent-minded air of people who know they are being watched.

Soon I found myself in an avenue which was empty and freshly watered, like a garden in the morning.

Nobody was shaking a duster out of the windows. Cars turned the street corners with care. The servants put on a jacket and hat when they went out. Everywhere there were the same entrances of gleaming black wood. From time to time an empty tram jumped over the dented rails. The street-lamps were taller than those in my neighbourhood.

It would soon be ten o'clock. I retraced my steps crossing on to the other pavement to get a different view.

I arrived at 6 rue Lord–Byron a few minutes before time. I always arrange to arrive early. In this way I have time to prepare myself.

Having passed in front of the door three or four times, I went in. Monsieur Lacaze's visiting card was in my pocket. I touched it only very occasionally in order not to dirty it. Finger-marks on anything white are so ugly. Cold drops of sweat rolled from my armpits all down my sides.

Through a glass door I saw a carpeted staircase.

The concierge, motionless in the middle of the courtyard, was looking at one of the windows.

I called him and he turned round.

'Monsieur Lacaze?' I enquired.

And to prove that I knew Monsieur Lacaze I held out his visiting card. I was proud because I was sure the rich manufacturer would not give his card to just any-body.

The concierge took the card. He was wearing a stiff cap. A feather-duster hung from his apron string.

'Are you the person with an appointment at ten o'clock?'

'Yes, I am.'

'Use the service stairs at the end of the courtyard. It's the second floor.'

As he did not give me back the card, I asked for it, because I thought it important.

'Here you are . . . take it.'

As I was crossing the courtyard I could feel him watching. That embarrassed me. I do not like people looking at my back when I walk. It makes me walk badly. I am conscious of my hands, of my heels and of my elevated shoulder.

When I was on the service stairs I breathed more freely.

A light bulb illuminated each landing and because it was daylight I could see the elements inside these bulbs. Even on this staircase there was an electric bell.

While I climbed the stairs I thought about the con-cierge. I could not believe Monsieur Lacaze had spoken to him about me. This concierge, certainly out of jealousy, had made me go up the service stairs. He had seen, with his practised servant's eye, that I was poor. If servants use their eyes in this way, it comes from their hating their jobs. They have renounced their in-dependence, but only as far as the rich are concerned. The instinct for freedom which in spite of everything exists at the bottom of their hearts enables them to distinguish at once between a rich man and a poor one, between one of the bosses and a man like themselves.

On the second floor I rang the bell. A maid opened the door. She must have been warned to expect me for, before I had time to speak, she solicitously asked me to go in.

I followed her. We went through the kitchen, which already smelled of hot fat, then along a long corridor.

Suddenly I found myself in an anteroom.

'Wait . . . I'll go and tell Monsieur Lacaze.'

Then I heard the manufacturer's voice through the dividing wall. He was saying,

'Show him in, the poor chap.'

I was offended. One does not like the servants to know what their master thinks of one. Besides, Monsieur Lacaze could surely not be unaware that I could hear him.

But as I am not familiar with the behaviour of rich people I was unwilling to take umbrage.

It could be that Monsieur Lacaze had more important things to occupy him than questions of self-esteem.

The maid reappeared. As she led me towards the office, she murmured,

'Don't worry . . . Monsieur Lacaze is very kind.'

I was blushing. The palms of my hands sweated. Stupefied by agitation, I moved towards the door, which was open and full of daylight, as a piece of wood is drawn into the centre of a whirlpool. I did not even think of trying to pull myself together. I said to myself,

'Let them do what they like with me.'

I went in.

The door closed behind me, silently. Two windows went right down to the floor: I could see the street from the middle of the room. I was dazzled. The only power that remained to me was to play up my awkwardness.

The edge of my ears burned, as they do when one has been very cold. My mouth was dry, because I had been breathing without salivating.

With my eyes wide open, the lashes raised, I looked at Monsieur Lacaze.

He was a different man. He had neither hat not overcoat. He was wearing black. A white parting divided his hair into two equal parts. From time to time his flat ears moved rapidly up and down.

At the station he had not made such an impression on me. I am used to seeing rich people outside. But here, standing up, touching his desk with the tips of his fingers, with his frock-coat with cloth-covered buttons, with his starched shirt which caused him no discomfort, he crushed me by his superiority.

'Sit down, my man.'

He had said that to me straight away, but I was so overcome that it seemed to me I had been standing up for a long time.

He looked at a gold watch whose slim hands gave as much importance to the minutes as the hours.

'Come on . . . sit down.'

I had understood, but my shyness prevented me from obeying. The armchairs were too low. Seated, I should have seemed his equal, which would have embarrassed me. And at the bottom of my heart, I felt that my remaining standing flattered him.

'Sit down, then . . . don't be afraid.'

I had to take several steps to reach the chair he had pointed out with a gesture of his hand.

I sat down and my body sank down even further than I had expected. My knees were too high. My elbows slipped on the rounded arms.

I tried very hard not to rest my neck on the back of the chair, that would have been showing too much familiarity. But my neck got tired, as it does when you raise your head in bed.

My hat on my knees smelled of damp hair. My eyes skimmed the level of the table, like those of a surveyor. Monsieur Lacaze was fiddling with a paper-knife, turning it over and over. I could see his forearm up to the elbow inside his cuff. Under the desk his legs were crossed. The one that did not touch the floor was trembling. The sole of his shoe was new, scarcely whitened in the centre.

'Well my man, I have brought you here because I take an interest in poor people.'

I changed my position. No creaking of springs came from the armchair.

'Yes, I take an interest in poor people, the really poor, of course. I detest those who take advantage of other people's kindness.'

Supporting himself on the desk, he got up like someone whose knees are painful, then he strode up and down the room with his hands behind his back, clicking two fingers like a Spanish dancer.

My head was on a level with his stomach. Embarrassed, I raised my eyes to look him in the face.

'I love the poor, my man. They are unfortunate. Every time I have an opportunity to come to their aid, I do so. You yourself seem to me to be in an interesting situation.'

'Oh, sir!'

On the mantelpiece three gilt horses were drinking a mirror in a gilt trough.

'Your show of consideration pleased me very much.'

'Oh, sir.'

I was feeling very pleased with the way the conversation was going when the door opened. A girl appeared and, noticing me, hestitated to come in. She was fair and pretty, like those women who are shown kissing horses' noses on English post-cards.

'Come in, Jeanne.'

I got up with some difficulty.

'Don't get up . . . don't get up . . .' said the manufacturer.

I was humiliated by this command. Monsieur Lacaze
had only told me to remain seated to make it clear to
me that I had nothing to do with his family.

He sat down at his desk and wrote something. The
girl waited and from time to time she glanced stealthily
at me.

Our eyes met. Immediately she turned away her
head.

I felt that for her I was a being from another world.
She was watching me in order to find out what sort of
creature I was, in the same way as she would have
watched a prostitute or a murderer.

At last she withdrew, a piece of paper in her hand.
She managed to take another look at me as she closed
the door.

'Were you in the army?'

'Yes, I was.'

I showed my injured hand.

'Ah, you were wounded; in the war, I hope.'

'Yes.'

'So you draw a pension?'

'Yes, sir . . . three hundred francs a quarter.'

'So that's invalidity benefit at fifty per cent.'

'Yes.'

'Do you have a job?'

'No, I don't.'

I added immediately:

'But I'm looking for one.'

'Your case is interesting. I'll do something for you.
But meanwhile, here you are.'

Monsieur Lacaze got out his wallet.

I shivered so violently that I felt as if my scalp were creasing.

How much was he going to give me? A thousand francs perhaps!

He counted the notes, which were pinned together, as one flicks through the pages of a book. I followed every movement.

He took out the pin and passed me a hundred franc note, having first rubbed it between his fingers to make sure there was only one.

I took it. I was embarrassed at keeping it in my hand and I did not dare put it in my pocket straight away.

'Come on, put it away, and above all don't lose it. You must buy a second-hand suit. Yours is too big.'

'Very well.'

'And then come and see me in your new suit.'

While Monsieur Lacaze was speaking, I was thinking I ought not to have been so quick to take the note. My attitude no longer fitted in with the way I had behaved at the station.

'Come and see me . . .'

The manufacturer, pausing on the word 'me', looked at his diary.

'Come and see me the day after tomorrow, at the same time. I shall be expecting you.'

He wrote something down. Then he asked:

'By the way, what is your name?'

'Bâton, Victor.'

Having noted down my name and address, he rang the bell.

The maid showed me out.

'Was he nice?' she asked.

'Yes.'

'Did he tell you to come back?'

'Yes.'

'That's because your case is interesting.'

III

The street was quiet. The sun could not be seen, though its presence could be felt. The pavement, which would be in the shade as soon as the sky cleared, was cooler.

I walked quickly in order to be more on my own and to be able to think.

Monsieur Lacaze had impressed me not only by his wealth but because he was kind. Things had not turned out as I had imagined during the night. That is how it always is. I know it but it is useless for me to try and stop myself picturing how things will be, because my imagination always gets the upper hand.

Some of the things the manufacturer had said had annoyed me, but after all he did not know me. Perhaps I too had annoyed him.

Rich people are not like us. I suppose they do not pay so much attention to details.

It was eleven o'clock. The prospect of going back to my own district was not inviting. I had some money. Why should I not go to Montmartre and have a drink and a good meal and forget my loneliness, sadness and poverty for a few hours?

At midday I reached the outer boulevards. I was hungry and to increase my hunger still further I purposely strolled about a bit.

Scraggy trees, leafless and without bark, tied to stakes, planted in holes with no railings, stood in a row, fifty yards apart. In each space there was one of those brown benches on which one has to sit up straight. Here and there were an empty stall, a urinal covered with pre-war advertisements, a foreigner unfolding a plan or consulting a Baedeker, which could be recognized by its spine.

I stopped in front of each restaurant to read the duplicated menu, stuck on to a window-pane.

Finally I went into a restaurant half-concealed behind barrels of shrubs.

The legs of the tables could not be seen because of the cloths. There were a lot of people there, and mirrors reflecting each other until they became too small to see, hats at an angle on the coat-racks and a cashier on an excessively tall stool.

I sat down. The cruet, the menu propped up between two glasses, a cut-glass carafe and a bread-basket were all within my reach.

Opposite me a man who nevertheless looked respectable was drawing naked women in order to have the pleasure of blackening in a triangle in the middle. Further off a woman was cleaning her nails with a pin; I could not have done that myself.

'Rose, the bill!' called a customer whose voice seemed strange to me, no doubt because I had never heard it before.

The waitress went towards him, with her white apron, a pencil in her hair and scissors for grapes.

I looked at her. Her legs disappeared under her skirt. Her breasts were too low. Her bosom was paler at the edge of her bodice. When she went away, removing the dirty plates, her body seemed more accessible, the nape of her neck more familiar, because I was seeing her from behind.

At last she turned her attention to me. She brought me one after another a bottle of wine, a sardine without a head, a slice of meat with a bit of string on it and some mashed potato striped with a fork.

A new customer settled himself beside me. I had to eat with my elbows squeezed against my body, which I did not like. He ordered a bottle of Vichy water. He wrote his name on the label because he was not going to drink all of it on the same day.

A tramp entered the restaurant, but he did not have time to ask for anything because the waitress chased him away with her tea-towel, just as, when she was a girl on the farm, she had frightened the geese by waving her arms.

My plate, which I had wiped with a piece of bread, shone greasily.

I called out, as I had heard other people doing:
'Rose, the bill!'

The waitress pencilled in some figures on the back of a menu, then, while she gave me my change, held the note I had given her between her teeth.

Although I was a bit drunk, I went out as awkwardly as a naked man.

After I had bought some *High Life* cigarettes which, in spite of their name, only cost a franc, I went into a bar.

A small amount of steam hissed as it rose from a nickel percolator. A waiter wrapped in a white apron was wiping away the marks left by the glasses on the tables with a cloth. The spoons knocked against the thick cups, sounding like counterfeit money.

As I like seeing my profile, I settled myself where I could see my image in one mirror reflected in another.

Four women were smoking at one table. They were wearing blouses coloured with packets of dye. One of them had one of those coats you blow on to find out if they are otter fur.

Just then she rose and, with her coat open and her cigarette between two straight fingers, came towards me. The heels of her shoes were too high. She came forward like somebody walking on her toes.

She sat down near me.

Her mouth looked as if it had been drawn on her skin, the outline was so precise. Her face-powder, which was thick round the nostrils, smelled pleasant. She had a speck of gold from the end of her cigarette on her lips.

She crossed her legs easily, like a man. I noticed that her white stockings were black over her ankle bones.

'Well, dearie, what are you going to get me?'

After all, for once I might as well forget my worries and enjoy myself.

'Whatever you like.'

The waiter, who did not seem to find this woman's behaviour at all odd, came up.

'A Benedictine, Ernest.'

'Right. And you, sir?'

'Nothing, thank you . . . I've already had a coffee,' and I pointed out my cup.

'Come on . . . do have something with me . . . darling.'

'Yes . . . if you want . . . A Benedictine.'

When my neighbour had drunk her liqueur, she got up and, having fetched her hat from where she had been sitting before, asked me to wait.

I waited until six o'clock. She did not come back: she had been making fun of me.

I called the waiter and while I paid I explained to him, although he had not asked, that a severe headache had obliged me to remain there.

Then I went out. It was only after I had been wandering about near the bar for half an hour that I managed to get away from it.

Night was falling. The air was heavy. The streets

smelled of tarmac, as they do when they are under repair. I had the disagreeable feeling that I was leaving the table just as people were getting ready to sit down.

IV

In the window of a baker's shop I had read a notice
which said:
>Black suit for sale because of owner's death:
>trousers, jacket, waistcoat. Enquire within.

The next day, being afraid that the notice might
have been taken down, I got up early.

When I went into the bakery the proprietor, whom I
could see in his entirety as his back was reflected in a
mirror, asked me what I wanted, like a shopkeeper
who was not prepared to wait for me.

'I've come about the suit.'

'Right.'

He called his wife who was putting some fancy
loaves on end. Although she was very fat she had a belt
round her waist.

She came forward, her knees all dusty with flour.

'The gentleman has come about the suit,' explained
the baker.

His wife was about to tell me what I needed to know
when a customer came in.

She abandoned me in order to serve him, while her
husband slid the coins on the marble counter into an
open drawer — as one might trap a fly.

One section of this drawer was filled with an untidy
pile of bank-notes. Smoothing them out and counting
them in the evening when the shop is closed must give
great pleasure.

'What is the person selling the suit called?' I asked.

'Junod. She's a widow.'

I was highly delighted to hear that this person was a widow. I prefer to do business with women than with men.

'And she lives at number 23.'

'Thank you.'

I could not go straight to the door because there was a girl crouching on the floor, washing the square flags.

The house which bore the number 23 had balconies which gave it a middle-class air.

I felt for my wallet. I always take this precaution before I buy anything and even sometimes when I am not buying anything.

Under the porch was a thick damp mat to wipe one's feet on and further on in the shadow a glass door which did not open from the outside.

'Concierge!'

A voice from the stairs called out:

'Here.'

'Madame Junod?' I enquired politely.

'What have you come about?'

'The suit.'

'Second floor, the door on the left.'

The wall of the staircase was painted to look like marble. The old wooden steps were polished.

On the first floor I read: mezzanine; on the second: first.

As I had counted two storeys, I stopped. At the left-hand door a bell-cord hung down to the keyhole. I pulled it gently, as it did not look very strong.

A bell tinkled, not directly behind the wall, but far away in the flat. Then someone closed a door — the kitchen door, probably.

A man appeared, hatless and without a tie. I thought

he looked as if he had been taken by surprise. As I looked at him I wondered what he had been doing before I rang his bell.

'I've come about the suit,' I said at last.

'What suit?'

'I saw a notice in the . . .'

'That's the floor above. The concierge ought to have told you.'

He pointed at the ceiling with his forefinger.

'The concierge told me it was the second floor.'

'This is the first floor . . . can't you read?'

I apologized and went up another storey. This time I made no mistake. Madame Junod's card was nailed to a door. The address had been crossed out with ink.

I rang. An ugly little woman with neatly done hair opened the door. A wedding-ring sat loosely on the skinny joint of one of her fingers. It is odd how ugly women's wedding-rings are particularly noticeable.

'I've come about the suit.'

'Oh! . . . come in . . . come in.'

This invitation pleased me. People who trust me are so unusual.

I wiped my feet very carefully as I always do when I visit anyone for the first time. I took off my hat and followed the woman.

She showed me into a dining-room. I stood in the middle, a long way from anything which might possibly be stolen.

'Do sit down.'

'Thank you . . . thank you.'

'So, you've come about the suit.'

'Yes . . . I have.'

'Oh, if only you knew how much it costs me to part with my poor husband's things! He died in his prime. If he knew that I had been forced to sell his clothes in order to live . . .'

I like it when people confide in me, just as I like it when I hear gossip about people. It makes conversation more lively.

'What can be more painful than to sell objects you have lived with and are as familiar with as the beauty-spots on your body!'

'That's true . . . one clings to memories,' I said, raising my hand.

'Especially to memories which bring back so much. Ah, if I could, I would keep this suit. It suited my husband so well. My poor husband was exactly your height. Perhaps he was a bit better built. He certainly was a real man. He was in charge of an office. You must have read his card on the door.'

'I didn't notice it.'

'The address was crossed out because we had the cards printed before we moved here. Yes, this suit brings back a lot of memories. My husband and I went to buy it together at Réaumur. I have kept the bill. I'll give it to you. It was an afternoon in the spring. People were looking to see if there were buds on the trees. The sun lit up the whole sky. A month later, my husband was dying. He had worn this suit twice, on two Sundays.'

'Only twice?'

'Yes. A suit that cost a hundred and sixty francs in 1916. At that time money was worth more than it is now. It is a proper suit. There are the trousers, the jacket and the waistcoat. Wait, I'll go and fetch it.'

Madame Junod came back a few moments later with the suit wrapped in a piece of cloth.

She put it down on the table, removed the pins and, taking the jacket, showed it to me front and back, on her outstretched arm.

I touched the fabric.

'Look at the lining.'

The suit really was new. There were no stains under

the arms. The buttonholes and pockets were stiff.

'It's heart-breaking for me to have to part with these relics. I'm afraid my husband, who is in heaven, may see me. But in any case I am not rich. I have to live. My husband will forgive me. Look, you see, there we are.'

She pointed out a photograph three-feet high which showed a married couple.

'You see it's an enlargement of an enlargement. The bigger my husband is, the more he seems to be alive.' I looked carefully at the couple. I could not recognize Madame Junod.

'Yes, that's really us, in 1915. The next day we were going off into the country.'

She looked me up and down from head to foot.

'He was your height, but rather better built.'

I thought that if he had been fatter, the suit would not fit me. But I was too tactful to voice my fears.

'In 1914, we were already engaged. Oh, those evenings beside the Seine. It was too hot in Paris. And because of the war, everybody put obstacles in our way.'

'But your husband wasn't a soldier.'

'Oh, but just think. He wasn't strong. And he, who ought to have lived because he wasn't a soldier, was carried off by sickness.'

'That's life,' I murmured.

'Yes, that's how the world goes.'

'But what did he die of?' I asked, suddenly afraid that it might have been a contagious illness.

'A stroke.'

Taking advantage of what she was reflecting on, I asked the price of the suit.

'It isn't dear; seventy-five francs. Just look at the cut.'

She drew her hand round in a semi-circle which no doubt indicated an imaginary figure.

'Feel the cloth. It's a pre-war English fabric. You can check for yourself. Even in the biggest shops you won't find cloth like that.'

I walked quickly past the lodge, embarrassed because the concierge knew there was a suit in the parcel under my arm.

A voice called out to me.

I turned. The concierge, who had been lying in wait for me, was there near the staircase.

'The gentleman on the first floor complained. I did tell you Madame Junod lived on the second floor. You must be careful. It's me the tenants hold responsible.'

Not wanting to provoke a scene, I left without allowing myself to get angry.

Because of my suit, I did not go and eat at Lucie's; she would have made fun of me.

I had lunch in one of those little restaurants where the menu is chalked up on a slate and then, to pass the time, I walked around the streets.

The jacket was a bit tight under the arms. The sleeves were too long and tickled my hands. The trousers fitted too tightly round my thighs. But the black suited me.

With my overcoat open, I looked at myself in all the shop-windows, without seeming to. I have noticed that I look much better in windows than in real mirrors.

When I felt that I had digested my meal, I went to the public baths. I knew there was one side for men and another for women. But for that I should not have gone in.

The cashier gave me a number. Nevertheless I was on my own.

The attendant did not take long to call me.

I went into a cubicle. The door did not lock. This worried me all through my bath, especially when I heard footsteps.

Since my feet were cold, the warmth of the water was very pleasant to me.

I soaped myself with a little piece of soap which could not sink, being careful to avoid my eyes. I entertained myself by floating.

As the water was getting cold, I jumped out and dried myself — starting with my face — on a towel which got wet as quickly as a handkerchief.

When I left the baths I felt so good that I made myself a promise to go back every time I had any money.

V

It was exactly ten o'clock when I arrived at Monsieur Lacaze's house.

I had put on my fine suit again and for the first time that year, I went without an overcoat.

I went into the office with more confidence than the day before.

The industrialist was chatting to his daughter. He seemed surprised to see me.

'Sit down,' he said, 'I'll be with you in a minute.'

He had forgotten that the day before yesterday he had addressed me formally. Then, speaking to the maid:

'I've told you twenty times not to show anyone in without warning me.'

'So you can't come today?' asked the girl, as soon as I was seated.

'No, dear.'

'And tomorrow?'

'But you aren't free!'

'Yes I am, after four o'clock. I come out of the Conservatoire at four o'clock.'

'I can't. Saturday, if you like.'

'All right.'

Having kissed her father, the girl went out. As she had done before, she glanced at me as she closed the door. Although it came from a long way off, the look disturbed me.

'So, my man, did you buy the suit?'

'Yes.'

'Good. Stand up.'

I obeyed, a bit embarrassed at not having an overcoat.

'Turn round.'

I did so, raising the shoulder which was too low.

'It fits you very well. You would think it had been made to measure. How much did you pay for it?'

'A hundred francs.'

'That's not dear. Now I can send you to my factory. You look presentable. I can recommend you to the personnel officer.'

Monsieur Lacaze unscrewed a fountain-pen, shook it and wrote a few lines on a visiting-card.

So that he should not suspect me of reading over his shoulder, I moved conspicuously away.

'Here you are,' cried the manufacturer, looking at the card sideways to see if the ink was dry.

I put the card in my wallet without reading it and sat down, hoping Monsieur Lacaze would busy himself with me and ask me questions.

Today when I was less overwhelmed I felt capable of replying intelligently and so of making myself interesting.

'So good-bye, my dear Bâ . . . Bâ . . . Bâton. That's all for today. Tomorrow morning, at seven o'clock go to my factory, 97 to 125, rue de la Victoire, at Billancourt. Ask for Monsieur Carpeaux. He will give you work. When you have a day off, just come and see me. Well, good-bye, my man.'

Disappointed at the brevity of this interview I stood up.

'Good-bye. Thank you very much.'

'Yes, good-bye, I'll see you sometime.'

I backed out, bowing, with my hat held flat against my chest.

VI

At dawn I went off to the nearest tram stop.

The wind was blowing so strongly that the front door of my house banged shut by itself before I had time to close it. Raindrops bigger than the rest dropped from the cornices on to my hands. The rain streamed over the pavements towards the road. Every time I crossed a street the water in the gutter, which was too wide to step across, swamped one of my feet. The water which was rushing down the drainpipes attached to the houses flowed over the ground as if a bucket had been knocked over. It did not take long for the sleeves of my jacket to make my shirt cuffs wet. My hands felt as if they had not been dried after a wash.

An empty tram arrived. It had been washed during the night. The lamps which lit it seemed sad like the light one has forgotten to put out before going to sleep.

I sat down in a corner. The heaters were still cold. A draught making its way under a seat chilled my hands. The conductress, motionless in the centre of the tram, was yawning.

'La Motte-Piquet!' she called.

She would have called out just the same even if the train had been empty.

We set off again. The doors opened all by themselves on bends. Sometimes the lights went out for a second. Behind the wet windows the streets trembled as they would in heat-haze.

'Grenelle.'

Some workmen got in. The dull sound of a bell rang

in the driver's ear. I thought about my unmade bed, still warm at the foot, about my closed window and this dawn which on other days I saw breaking between my eyelashes as I slept.

At that moment, in the light from his open door, Monsieur Lecoin must be washing.

'Pont Mirabeau!'

Two men came and sat opposite me.

I was furious because there was room elsewhere. They were talking as if it were midday.

'Avenue de Versailles!'

A workman got in with an unfolded newspaper, whose news seemed much too fresh.

Day was breaking. Suddenly the tram lights went out. Everything changed colour. Through the grey-framed windows the rain could be seen.

'Chardon-Lagache!'

I felt sad and alone. All these people knew where they were going. As for me, I was setting out on an adventure.

'Point-du-Jour!'

I got out. A stream of water falling from the roof of the tram went down my back. My legs, shaken by the shuddering of the tram, were giving way. My face, which had been motionless for a long time, was stiff. My left foot was cold.

The tram went away, carrying off the heads I had got to know, and my empty place.

In a hut, two customs officers who had not had any sleep were getting ready to leave.

To get to Billancourt, you have to go out of Paris.

I went along an avenue without a pavement, which had low houses on either side.

It was still raining. The mud, which was sticking to my shoes, squelched at every footstep. Behind a wall a tree was stirring like a thicket with someone in it. The wind was blowing the leaves upside-down. The rain was making bubbles on the puddles.

Monsieur Lacaze's factory was surrounded by a wall. If you looked up you could see smoking chimneys of varying height.

'Monsieur Carpeaux?' I asked the porter.

'Monsieur Henri, you mean.'

'Yes.'

The watchman closed the door of his cabin carefully — I can never see the point of it — and, before he left, imagining himself a stranger, tried to open it.

'Follow me,' he said, without looking at me.

He wanted to understand that he was not taking me to Monsieur Carpeaux out of kindness, but because it was his job.

He stopped in front of a building vibrating with machinery.

Without bothering about me, he chatted to a workman. Then, suddenly, as if it were not on my account that he was there, he said:

'It's for Monsieur Henri.'

I was shown into a white wooden room. Its walls were covered with advertisements for tyres.

Soon Monsieur Carpeaux appeared.

Contrary to what I had imagined, he was a young man with a sparse moustache like that of women, when they have one. He wore glasses the colour of tincture of iodine.

I handed him Monsieur Lacaze's card, on which these words had been written:

Dear Carpeaux,

I am sending you a good chap; give him work.

'Oh, Monsieur Lacaze has sent you.'

'Yes.'

'Right. Wait a moment.'

He disappeared and came back a few minutes later.

'That's settled,' he said; 'you will start work on Monday.'

'Thank you very much.'

'Monday, at seven o'clock.'

'Thank you, thank you, but you know I can't use my left hand. I was wounded.'

'Well, you don't need your left hand to write.'

'I know, but I wanted to tell you.'

'Yes, I understand. Till Monday, then.'

VII

The days are long when there is nothing to do, especially if one has only a few francs.

As I had got used to my suit (its lapels had been put out of shape by the rain and the trousers were stained with mud at the back of the legs), I was able to go and eat at Lucie's.

In the army, when you are not there for a meal, they put your share to one side. The same thing happens at Lucie's.

So I had a very good lunch.

When I left the restaurant it was no longer raining.

I was going in the direction of the Palais de Justice when an idea which came to me, I do not know quite how, overwhelmed me. I stopped breathing. My heart pounded in my chest. I no longer noticed that my feet were wet at the edge of the sole.

I had just had the idea of going to wait for Monsieur Lacaze's daughter when she came out of the Conservatoire.

I struggled feebly against this whim for a few minutes. It was no good. The prospect of speaking to a rich girl was too attractive. That rainy afternoon it was like a meeting one had been waiting for for several days. It was the unknown, perhaps love. I was not drawn to the girl by any physical desire. Indeed, when I fall in love with anyone, I never think about possessing her. I find that the longer that is delayed, the more delightful it is.

I wandered about the streets, with my soul absorbed in its own blind happiness. People's closed umbrellas were still glistening wet. The pavements were growing paler beside the walls.

Above the door of the Conservatoire there was a flag.

It was only a quarter to four.

In order to contain my impatience, I went for a bit of a walk and thought of all the wonderful things that would happen if Mademoiselle Lacaze loved me. You must not think that I had her wealth in mind. If she were to offer me money, I knew very well that I should refuse indignantly. When she came to my wretched room, I should be worthy of her.

Nevertheless I must admit that if she had been poor my love would have vanished. I do not understand that.

Suddenly a porter opened the second side of the double door of the Conservatoire.

A minute later the girl came running out like a traveller who wants to be the first to give up her ticket.

My blood pounded in my temples and wrists. There I felt it was knotting my veins.

As Mademoiselle Lacaze passed close by me, her eyes met mine. Her lips moved. She had recognized me. However, she did not speak to me.

I followed her. She was indeed beautiful with her hair hanging down her back and her short skirt.

I walked quickly, ready to slow down if she should turn round.

Soon I overtook her and, raising my hat, I greeted her.

She did not reply.

Now I was in front of her and, in order that she should catch me up, I stopped to light a cigarette.

A man from a good family whom I had known in

the army had told me that the way to pick up women was to ask for permission to accompany them. I was getting ready to put this advice into practice but, as she did not catch me up, I turned round.

She was no longer there.

VIII

The next morning I awoke with a start.

Someone had knocked on my door so violently that it made a sound like thunder, as if a full packing-case had been dropped.

At first, I thought I was dreaming. But the knocking was renewed.

I leapt out of bed. My fright stopped me from feeling the cold which crept up under my shirt.

'Who's there?' I asked quietly, as if I were still asleep.

'It's me, Lacaze.'

Saying his name out loud, behind a door, caused *him* no embarrassment.

I looked through the keyhole, expecting to see an eye without lashes, without an eye-lid.

But why should Monsieur Lacaze come to see me? Perhaps he wanted to check up on what I had told him; perhaps he was about to give me some good news.

The knocking came again.

I could have opened the door, but when I am not dressed I feel weak.

'Wait . . . just a second.'

I opened the window to let in some fresh air. I opened it without making any noise so that the manufacturer should not be aware of it.

I put on my trousers and jacket and wiped my face with the corner of a damp towel.

Then I closed the window quietly.

With my shirt not tucked down properly into my trousers, I opened the door.

Monsieur Lacaze came in without taking off his hat. His rattan walking-stick, which he held behind him, knocked into the furniture as he turned.

'You are a nasty piece of work,' he said, stopping close to me.

He knew everything: I was lost. Not knowing what attitude to adopt, I feigned ignorance.

'You deserve a thrashing. You have no shame: following a young girl . . . with her hair down her back.'

I mumbled, unable to find any excuse.

'Look what reward you get when you do good . . . I gave you money . . . I found you a job in my factory . . . thanks . . .'

He was so angry I was afraid he would hit me. I could scarcely believe that I was the cause of such anger.

'Yes . . . look at the thanks I get. Look out for yourself, the police will have something to say to you. You are a miserable specimen . . .'

He went out at last, banging the door so hard that it did not close properly.

I could hear his footsteps on the stairs and when the sound changed on the landings I was afraid he was coming back.

Sitting on the bed I looked at my new suit, for which there was no longer any purpose, and at my untidy room in the chilly morning air.

I had a raging headache. I pondered my dreary life, with no friends and no money. I only asked to be allowed to love, to be like everybody else. It was not much to ask.

Then suddenly I broke into sobs.

Soon I realized that I was making myself cry.

I stood up. The tears dried on my cheeks.

I had the unpleasant feeling you get when you have washed your face and have not wiped it dry.

Blanche

Blanche

I

When I have a bit of money I go for an evening walk in the rue de la Gaîté.

This street smells of cooking and scent at the same time.

Cakes cost less there than elsewhere. There are stoves with pancakes cooking three at a time. People have to keep stepping off the pavement because of the crowds. Halfway down the street is a police station where the officers do not wear caps and there are bicycles at the door. In the photographers' shops there are heads repeated a dozen times on a strip which looks as if it has been cut from a film. A stationer sells songs with music and postcards showing the monuments of Paris in summer.

One evening I was looking at a cinema advertisement gleaming under its layer of paste. Some vandal or other had drawn a cigarette in the heroine's mouth. I was lamenting people's stupidity, when my eyes fell upon a woman who was looking me up and down without my noticing.

Guessing that she had been watching me, I made a mental summary of what I had just been doing, in order to reassure myself that I had not been doing anything unbecoming.

I was pleased. It is pleasant to be watched without knowing it, especially when one looks as if one is not paying attention. Once I recognized myself in a photograph in a newspaper, among a crowd. That gave me more pleasure than the finest studio enlargement.

The woman was not smartly dressed, because of her feet; but a woman only has to look at me for me to find her attractive.

As I am shy, I had to struggle not to lower my eyes. A man ought not to be the first to lower his eyes.

A man with a little white beard and a hat over his eyes was looking at the woman too. He had stopped. He was shifting his weight from one leg to the other, like a wading bird.

Being afraid I might get in before him, he went up to the unknown woman, took off his hat like something which must not be upset and mumbled some words I could not hear.

I looked at him from behind. He must be laughing or talking, because the ends of his moustache were moving. Oh, if I had been in that woman's place, how I should have slapped his face.

She did not slap him, but she turned away. Taken aback, the man put his hat on his head and did not let go of it until it was back in its former position, then, moving some distance away, he pretended to do up his shoelace.

In my turn I went up to the unknown woman. Men are so vain that even if they see a woman turn away ten suitors they will still pay court to her themselves.

'Excuse me.'

I took care not to wink.

'I expect that man was being offensive. I'm speaking to you so that he doesn't bother you.'

'Thank you.'

She raised her head. Her eyes and ears were half hidden by her hat. She had a regular nose, pale lips which, when she half opened her mouth, stayed stuck together at the corners and on her chin a round beauty-spot.

'These old men are really very rude.'

'Yes, they are . . . what did he say to you?'

It was less out of curiosity than to prolong the pleasure of having been preferred that I asked my neighbour this question.

'He said something obscene.'

I wanted to ask what it was but I did not dare.

'Something obscene?'

'Yes, he said something obscene.'

I thought as much. I often notice these fresh-faced old men, smelling of lavender, gadding about the streets. They devote twenty francs a day to women. They are free until ten o'clock. They do whatever they like, because their private life is no one else's business.

'Let's get away from here, if you don't mind.'

'Yes . . . yes.'

I glanced furtively at my companion's feet, to see if she was wearing good shoes.

It is very odd that, beside her, I experienced the strange feeling I had had beside a civilian, when I had been in the army. Her skirt, her fur wrap, her hat, had a smell of freedom about them. Her clothes were only clothes. She did not have to be familiar with all their stains and creases.

I would have been completely happy if I had not been afraid something odd might suddenly happen. Women are so strange. My neighbour was quite capable of suddenly saying good-bye at the corner of a street.

As we did not know each other, we talked about the old man for half an hour.

At last, as I could not think of anything else to say on that subject, I asked:

'Perhaps you are on the stage.'

'I am a singer.'

'A singer?'

'Yes.'

Thinking that I was dealing with a famous actress, I wanted to know what she was called.

'What's your name?'

'Blanche de Myrtha.'

'Myrtha?'

'Yes, with a γ.'

'It's a stage name, I suppose?'

'I am called Blanche, but I invented de Myrtha.'

I racked my memory, hoping to remember having seen this cumbersome stage name somewhere.

'Don't let's go far. I'm due on at the Trois Mousquetaires at five past ten. You can just have a beer while you wait for me.'

In my imagination I saw myself living with this woman in a luxurious flat. I had some pyjamas and some slippers, with clean soles that glided over the carpets.

'Do you live by yourself?' I asked straightaway, in order not to foster any illusions, if she did not.

'Yes.'

'So do I.'

She looked at a mirror stuck on to the inside of her compact, and powdered her cheeks with a tiny powder-puff.

'Just a minute, let's go down this street; we'll be able to talk in peace there.'

The street was lit by blue glass lamps and the illuminated signs of hotels. From time to time a man and woman, not arm in arm, disappeared down a passageway.

Blanche's arm, long and soft like an animal's back, warmed my fingers. Her hat brushed against my ear. Our hips touched.

I was happy. Nevertheless my happiness was marred by absurd thoughts.

What would Blanche have done if we had met her best friend? Would she have left me? Or what if a sudden pain prevented her from walking? Or if she had even broken a window, or torn her skirt or jostled a passer-by?

I sometimes wonder if I am not mad. I had every reason to be happy and yet these senseless thoughts had to come and disturb me.

Whenever a man crossed the street and drew near us, my heart thumped. I know what it was: I wanted to be alone in the world with my companion.

I let go of her arm and laid my hand on her waist, very lightly, so I could take it away before she got annoyed if she did not like it.

She did not get angry.

Then my only thought was to kiss her, but I dared not do it while we were walking, for fear of missing her mouth.

'Let's stop. I want to say something to you.'

My voice trembled. I took her hands and smoothed my lips with my teeth.

'What do you want to say?'

I clasped her to me. Our knees knocked together like wooden balls. I took care not to lose my balance and not to step on her toes.

Then, suddenly, I kissed her.

As I straightened up, I felt that my hat was pushing hers out of place.

Although she quickly put it back over her eyes, I realized that it had annoyed her.

Abashed, with my arms dangling, I did not know whether I ought to kiss her again or apologize.

A woman, young and beautiful, passed close to us, in a fur coat. I blushed, because I realized Blanche was jealous. I could not say why envy is such an ugly thing in a woman.

'Look, it must be ten o'clock. I must go and sing.'

'Yes . . . but . . .'

'But?'

'I should like to kiss you again, without hats this time.'

'Yes, if you like.'

We kissed slowly, with our heads bare. I did not recognize Blanche's eyes, so close to mine.

She pushed me gently away.

'Let's be quick. I shall be late.'

Close together like a couple under an umbrella we retraced our steps.

The Trois Mousquetaires café was full. A comedian was singing on a platform of white wood. There were posters showing the singer de Myrtha.

While Blanche was making for a door on which 'Private: Artistes only' was written in chalk, I sat down.

The customers looked at me with admiration, thinking I was the singer's lover.

A Breton tenor followed the comedian. The pianist, who, because of his long hair, had a handsome head, played the *Paimpolaise*.

Near me a rough-looking type was singing all by himself, with his head bent. Inside his sleeve, on his wrist, I could see half a tattoo. Further off, a woman was licking her fingers which were sticky with liqueur.

Then Blanche appeared on the platform. I thought she would look in my direction, but she did not.

She sang three songs, with one hand clasped in the other, and when she had finished she came down from the platform holding her skirt.

A few minutes later she joined me.

'Time to go home.'

'Do you live far away?'

'Yes, in the rue Lafayette, at the Modern Hotel.'

II

An hour later we were going into the hotel.

A man-servant was asleep in an armchair with his legs together as if they were tied up.

In the distance I could see myself in a mirror as I walked and, so that I could go on seeing myself, I got off the carpet.

The stairs were evidently lighted all night. A carpet, held in place by brass stair rods, made them look reasonably smart.

Blanche's room was untidy. A handkerchief was drying on the heater. A blouse was hanging from the key of a cupboard.

In the middle of the ceiling there was a ring with no lamp hanging from it.

Not daring to sit down, not knowing what to do within those four walls, I wandered round the room and every time I passed the mirror-fronted wardrobe the overhanging boxes on top of it wobbled.

Blanche had difficulty in drawing the curtains: the rings were too high up and would not slide along the rails. At last she managed it.

Then, without bothering about me, she undressed: she was not nearly so striking in her chemise.

She cleaned her nails with the curved end of a hairpin. She washed, but in a very curious way.

Ever since she had been barefoot, she had been walking with shorter steps.

Suddenly she slipped between the sheets, having

first wiped the soles of her feet on the bed-side rug.

I woke up at dawn. A dim, ground-floor light was coming in through the window. It was raining. I could hear the drops falling on the paving-stones.

Blanche was asleep. She was taking up almost all the space in the bed.

Her nose and forehead were shiny. Her mouth was half-open, and her lips, because they were separated, did not seem to belong to the same mouth.

I missed my own bed. I would have liked to get up quietly, get dressed and go away, out into the rain, and leave that room which smelled of our breath and un-aired sheets.

It was beginning to get light. I could make out some clothes on a chair and some useless vases on the mantelpiece.

Suddenly, Blanche's eyelids lifted, revealing two dead eyes. She muttered a few words, moved her legs and instinctively pulled all the bed-clothes around her.

I got out of bed with my hair dishevelled and my shirt hanging down to my large knees.

I washed in cold water, without soap, and, still sleepy, went and stood at the window.

I saw a street I did not know, trams, umbrellas and big golden letters fixed up on a balcony.

The sky was grey and when I raised my head my forehead grew damp with drops of rain.

'Are you going, darling?'

'Yes.'

I dressed quickly.

'When can I see you again, Blanche?'

'I don't know.'

'Tomorrow?'

'If you like.'

I kissed my mistress on the forehead and went out.

The staircase smelled of chocolate. I saw a tray on the floor.

A minute later I was in the street.

I have never tried to see Blanche again.

I

The landlord has given me notice.

It seems that the tenants complained that I did not have a job. Nevertheless I lived very soberly. I went downstairs quietly. I was very obliging. When the old lady on the third floor had a heavy shopping-bag to carry, I helped her to take it up. I wiped my feet on the three mats which lay one after another before the stairs. I kept all the rules of the house which were posted up near the entrance. I did not spit on the stairs as Monsieur Lecoin did. In the evening, when I came home, I did not throw down the matches with which I had been lighting my way. And I paid my rent, yes, I paid it. It is true I had never given the concierge a tip, but all the same I did not give her much trouble. The only thing was that once or twice a week I used to come home after ten o'clock. Opening the door is nothing to a concierge. It can be done automatically, while asleep.

I lived on the sixth floor, a long way from the flats. I did not sing or laugh, out of tactfulness, because I did not work.

A man like me, who does not work, who does not want to work, will always be disliked.

In that house full of working people, I was the madman that, deep down, everyone wanted to be. I was the one who went without food, the cinema, warm clothes, to be free. I was the one who, without meaning to, daily reminded people of their wretched state.

People have not forgiven me for being free and for not being afraid of poverty.

The landlord has given me notice legally, on stamped paper.

My neighbours told him I was dirty, stuck-up, and perhaps even that women used to come to my room.

God knows how kind I am. God knows all the good deeds I have done.

Just as I remember a man who, when I was small, gave me a few sous, so lots of children will remember me when they have grown up because I often give them little presents.

It makes me extremely happy to know I shall always live in their hearts.

I am going to have to leave my room. Then is my life so abnormal as to give people offence? I cannot believe it.

In a fortnight I shall be somewhere else, I shall no longer have the key of this room where I have lived for three years, where I took off my army uniform, where, when I had been demobilised, I thought I was going to be happy.

Yes, in a fortnight I shall be leaving. Then perhaps the neighbours will be sorry, for changes always have some effect, even on the most unfeeling people. They will perhaps feel, even if only for a second, that they have done wrong. That will be enough for me.

They will come into my empty room and, as there will not be any furniture any more, they will look into the cupboards, but they will not see anything.

It is over. The sun will no longer show me the time on the wall. The invalid who lives on my landing will die a fortnight after my departure, for something new must happen. A bit of repainting will be done. Workmen will repair the roof.

It is strange how everything changes when you are not there.

II

I have been unable to find a room: so I have sold my furniture.

It is ten o'clock in the evening. I am alone in my hotel room.

It is wonderful to have got rid of my neighbours, to have gone, to have left Montrouge.

I look around for, after all, this is the room where I am going to live. I open the cupboard. There is nothing there except some newspaper on the shelves.

I open the window. The motionless air from a court-yard does not come in. Opposite, a shadow is passing and repassing behind a curtain. I can hear the iron wheels of a tram.

I come back to the middle of my room. Now wax is dripping from the strongly-burning candle and the motionless flame is no longer smoking.

A water-jug is stoppered with a folded towel. There is a carafe topped with a glass. The linoleum in front of the wash-stand has been discoloured by damp feet. The springs of the railed bed are gleaming. Voices which I do not know sound loudly on the staircase.

The plaster on the walls is white like the end of the sheet folded back over the bed-covers. Some unknown person is moving about in the adjoining room.

I sit on a chair — a folding garden chair — and think of the future.

I believe that one day I shall be happy, that one day someone will love me.

But I have been counting on the future for so long!

Then I go to bed — lying on my right for the sake of my heart.

The stiff sheets are so cold that I stretch out very cautiously. I am aware that the skin of my feet is rough.

I have of course locked the door. Nevertheless it seems to me that it is open, that somebody or other is about to come in. Luckily I have left the key in the keyhole: in this way nobody can get in with a second key.

I try to sleep but I think about my clothes, folded in the case, which must be getting creased.

My bed is warming up. I am not moving my feet in order not to catch the sheets because that makes me shiver.

I make sure that the ear I am lying on is nice and flat, that it is not folded.

Ears that stick out are so ugly.

Moving from my house has made me fidgety. I feel like moving about as I do when I imagine that I am tied up. But I fight against it: I must sleep.

My eyes, which are wide open, can see nothing, not even the window.

I think about death and the sky, for whenever I think about death, I think about the stars too.

I feel very small beside the infinite and quickly abandon these thoughts. My warm body, which is alive, reassures me. I touch my skin lovingly. I listen to my heart, but I take good care not to lay my hand on the left side of my chest for there is nothing which frightens me so much as that regular beat which I do not control and which could so easily stop. I move my joints and breathe more freely when I feel that they do not hurt.

Solitude, what a sad and beautiful thing it is! How beautiful when we choose it! How sad when it is forced upon us year after year!

Some strong men are not lonely when they are alone, but I, who am weak, am lonely when I have no friends.